TEAM PLAYERS

a novel by
Douglas Putnam

Printed and bound in the United States of America by
Maverick Publications • Bend, Oregon

"The group is a tyrant, so also is it a friend; *and it is both at once.*"

William H. Whyte, *The Organization Man.*

1

During session, Mary Lou Harkins, the Speaker of the House, stayed in a suite on the eleventh floor of the Union Plaza Hotel. It was there that Jack Preston, the gentleman from the 53rd District, went one day in April to receive his lashes for the mortal sin he had committed.

The Speaker said nothing as she opened the door.

"Good morning," Preston said.

She pointed at a chair next to a coffee table, and after Preston sat down, she went into the bedroom. He heard coughing, running water, the opening and shutting of drawers. In the picture window in front of him, the sun was huge, lighting the space with a brilliant glow. After several minutes, the Speaker came out of the bedroom and stood in the midst of it.

"Thank you for meeting me here so early," Preston said. "Instead of at your office, I mean. The entire world won't be gossiping about us."

"Not yet they won't."

Preston caressed a wooden pagoda the size of an upright shoebox on the coffee table. "This is exquisite," he said.

"Hand-carved teak," she said. "A gift from my friends at Honda. I keep it here to ward off evil spirits."

"Is it working?"

"What happened, Jack?"

"Excuse me?"

"You got loose with some babe reporter at some happy hour."

"No."

"And even though you tried like the devil to be a good boy, you couldn't keep your mouth shut."

"That isn't what happened."

"What did?"

"She pulled my financial disclosure form from the Secretary of State's office and saw the honorariums," Preston said. "She called me and asked about them. We got together and I explained what they are, how they work." He laid the pagoda back on the table. "She wrote up the interview and the *Athens News* ran it."

"Who do you think you are, partner?"

"If it hadn't been me, it would have been someone else."

"Cheap excuse."

"If not her, some other reporter."

"Cop-out."

"With all due respect Madame Speaker, you're too upset about this."

"Too upset my ass. You flat-out sucker punched me."

"I'm sorry."

"Opened a can of worms that doesn't need to be opened," she said. "The *Citizen* and *Plain Dealer* and *Beacon-Journal* will pounce on this."

"The bankers gave me five hundred dollars last month to eat breakfast with their legislative committee at the Capital Club," Preston said. "The homebuilders and school boards did, too."

"Maybe you're worth it."

"The people of this state have a right to know about those exchanges."

"The law doesn't require you to disclose any of that money."

"It's about transparency," Preston said. "I'm disclosing *more* than the law requires. Because it's the right thing to do."

"You're the expert on what's right?"

She turned away from him and went to the picture window. Below her, on Capitol Square, the hulking limestone Statehouse stood empty, surrounded by chain link fence, earthmovers, and mounds of dirt, closed for three years for extensive renovation after decades of neglect and haphazard maintenance.

"All of us in the House and Senate have an arrangement," the Speaker said. "It works well."

"I can see that."

"We only disclose income we receive during a year from any single source if it is *over* five hundred dollars."

"Yes, ma'am."

"We discussed this your first week in office," she said. "You seemed to be fine with it."

"I was—at that point."

"As of *right now*, the President of the Senate is fine with it. The lobbyists are fine with it. And I'm fine with it."

"Does anybody else get a vote?"

She twirled around from the window, scowled at Preston, and put her hands on her hips. "If you're so clean and pure, why do you take honorariums at all?"

"I don't claim to be clean and pure," Preston said. "I just want *everything* I get to be laid out in black and white. Clear enough for a ten-year-old to understand."

"Is that why you ran for public office? Is that what you want to accomplish here?"

"Yes."

"Crawl out of your sandbox and wipe your ass off," she said. "That's the silliest thing I've ever heard."

"There's nothing at all silly about it."

"We deal with *real* problems here," the Speaker said. "Millions of lives, billions of dollars. Some of us care more about *that* than we do about who's eating breakfast with you."

"No rep or senator should be allowed to get five hundred dollars a year under the radar. From *anybody*. It has to stop."

She was into his face now, leaning over him as he squirmed on his chair. "*Why* does it have to stop?" she said. "It takes *skill* to put together a budget, write laws, watchdog hundreds of agencies. Perot and the rest of his pinheads who hate government are wrong."

"Let's figure out why they hate it and maybe change some things."

"So are the yo-yos who passed term limits."

"Eight years and out isn't such a bad idea."

"Eight years and out is a crock of shit," she said. "The voters of my district can throw me out any time they want to."

"I didn't know you felt that strongly about it."

"And you know something else, partner? Honorariums are no big deal."

"If they're no big deal, why are you all hiding them?"

"Because the law says we can."

"Who wrote the law—you and Evan Breese?"

"Evan Breese doesn't write laws. *We* do."

"This is about politics, too," Preston said. "We're dealing with perceptions."

The Speaker went to the kitchenette and poured a cup of coffee for herself. "As long as we're on perceptions, I've got one of *you* I'm picking up from the guys." She snapped a swath of paper towel off the holder and began to wipe out the sink and toaster oven. "Arrogant, aloof, holier-than-thou."

"I'm aware of that."

"You've got this superiority complex, Jack. Like you're the only one who got into politics for the *right* reasons and the rest of us don't have a clue."

"I know I come off that way," Preston said.

"How does a guy who runs a coffee shop in Port Clinton get to thinking he's got the whole world figured out?"

"I'm trying to change."

"It's a shame because you've got potential."

"Thank you."

"You're enough of a butt-grinder to drag the bills back to the Holiday Inn every night and actually read them."

"I appreciate that."

"How many rookies do you think get a seat on Ways & Means?" she said.

"The old timers tell me I'm the first they can ever remember."

"I put you there because you've got a *brain*," she said. "But it's all going to go to waste if you keep on playing Lone Ranger."

"I'm working on my people skills."

She shut off the faucet in the sink, turned around and smirked at him. "Maybe you ought to head back up home and work on your people skills in your primary."

"I'll win my primary," Preston said. "Don't worry about that."

"Oh, I'm not *worried*," she said. "I really don't give a damn anymore if you win your primary or not. And once this story blows up, a lot of your colleagues are going to feel the same way."

"There are members of the caucus who support full disclosure," Preston said. "They're afraid to speak up."

"Who?"

"I won't tell you."

"Give me their names."

"No."

The Speaker balled up the paper towels and dropped them into the wastebasket. "Maybe we'll be better off if you *do* lose," she said. "Deak might be more loyal to the caucus than you've been."

"Deak is a slimeball and a thief. He's an embarrassment to our party."

"He might show more respect to the institution than you have."

"I am neither disloyal nor disrespectful."

"Don't count on any help from me," she said. "Not one damn dime."

"Because of this interview I just gave?"

"Yes."

"That's outrageous," Preston said. "I've been rock solid on every important issue—prevailing wage, worker's comp, collective bargaining. I've earned your support."

"Yes, you have."

"Ten times over."

"And you lost it because you didn't have enough sense to keep your mouth shut in front of your sexy reporter friend."

"You're funding Zinn," Preston said. "He's doing more damage to the caucus than I ever could."

"This has *nothing* to do with Zinn."

"Of course it does."

"Stop now."

"The crap he's pulling. Talk about disrespect to the institution. My God."

"I said stop."

"Zinn doesn't push the envelope. He pulverizes it."

At the sink, the Speaker sipped her coffee and studied Preston's face for a long moment. "Do you understand the situation we're in?"

"I think I do, yes."

"Marvelous. You've been so busy galloping around on your white horse, I wasn't sure if you were aware of the bigger picture."

"I assure you I am."

"Our majority is at risk in November," she said. "We're the only Democrats still standing in this town. Does that mean *anything* to you?"

"Absolutely."

She came at him hard across the floor, clutching her coffee cup with both hands in front of her. "Then start acting like it," she said. "If you think money runs this place *now*, see what happens if Torp takes over."

"I'll win my second term, with or without your help," Preston said. "I think you need to be worried about your own race."

The Speaker's jaw dropped. Her eyes narrowed, and the blood drained from her face. "What in the name of God would you know about *my* race?"

"Only what I hear," Preston said. "From people whose opinion I respect. They say you're vulnerable and you've got a fight on your hands."

"Every election is a fight."

"They tell me you've been in this business twenty years, that you're surrounded by yes men and losing touch," Preston said. "I think they may have a valid point."

"We're finished," the Speaker said. She moved toward the door of the suite. "Go save the world, Jack. From all us crooks in public office who don't know our heads from our asses."

"I'm sorry."

"You sure as hell are."

"If I upset you, I mean."

Preston left the suite. The Speaker flung her half-full coffee cup into the sink, went into the bedroom, and flopped onto the unmade bed. She lay for several minutes in silence and then a guttural, grinding noise exploded out of her mouth.

She went back into the outer room and picked up the hand-carved teak pagoda from her friends at Honda off the coffee table. In one quick motion, she hurled it over her head hard against the wall. It shattered into dozens of pieces.

She kicked off her shoes, got down on her knees, and began to pick them up off the carpet.

2

Two hours later, Evan Breese surfaced from the parking lot beneath the Statehouse and crossed High Street, heading toward the Center and his rendezvous with the Speaker.

He walked to the rear of the skyscraper, swiped a key card to pass through a door, nodded to a security guard, and entered a freight elevator that took him to the back kitchen and office area of Christopher's, the elegant restaurant on the thirty-first floor.

After greeting several workers, he went out to the main dining area. There, in a windowless alcove, shielded from the rest of the patrons, he found her—head down, pen in hand, poring over some document she'd pulled out of her satchel of reading material. Next to her on the table were the remnants of a fruit cup and a bowl of granola.

"Hello, sweetheart," Breese said. She raised her face up from her reading. He kissed her lightly on the forehead and sat down.

"What are you picking up?" she asked.

"This thing *could* turn into a monster," Breese said. "Maybe we should cut if off before it grows legs."

"But we can't. The son of a bitch blabbed and now they'll be coming after *us*."

"That doesn't exactly scare the bejesus out of me," Breese said.

"It should. It could be the end of everything—for you *and* me."

"Of all the piddly ass crap to get nailed on," Breese said. "Just shows how desperate these reporters are."

She looked at him with frightened eyes and grabbed his wrist so tightly that it hurt. "Stay with me, counselor," she said. "Don't desert me in my hour of need."

"I promise to protect you from all flak that comes your way," Breese said. "From Preston or anybody else."

"He was over to see me this morning," the Speaker said. "In his hippie glasses and rumbled tweed jacket and Earth shoes. Or whatever the hell they call them. Acting befuddled."

"Don't let the absent-minded professor routine fool you."

"Couldn't understand why I'm so upset."

"He's sharp as a tack."

"I know that. But he's got no concept of party loyalty."

"He may be a stealth R."

"Or worse," she said. "This creature may actually have voted for Perot. And term limits."

"Whatever he is, he's not one of us."

"And he won't be," she said. "Which is why I've decided to rip him a new asshole."

A spasm of fear rippled through Breese's chest. "Exactly *how* are you going to do that?"

"By giving fifty thousand to Deak."

A waiter came into the alcove and put a basket of pecan rolls on the table. Breese thanked him, thumbed through the selection, and popped one into his mouth. "When I said cut it off before it grows legs, that is *not* what I had in mind."

"As soon as possible."

"Pulling the plug on Preston is one thing," Breese said. "Fifty large to Deak on the down low is another. He'll never beat Preston."

She scoffed and waved a hand at him. "In three weeks, Nelson Mandela will be president of South Africa," she said. "Never say never."

"Preston may be in *your* doghouse, but he doesn't have a soul pissed off up in his district," Breese said. "Deak shouldn't bother getting in the ring with him because he has *no* chance."

"Be careful with your absolutes."

"Call him a ten-to-one underdog then. You don't back a ten-to-one underdog with fifty large."

"If he's running against Preston you do."

Breese shoved another pecan roll into his mouth. "Deak isn't exactly a quality human being," he said.

"Compared to who? A smart-ass who blabs?"

"You're going to need your money later," he said. "If you throw it away now in moment of rage, you're going to hate yourself down the road."

"I agree," she said. "That's why we need to use *your* money."

"I would prefer to stay out of that race," Breese said.

"I would prefer you do what I ask you to do."

"Don't go off half-cocked on this. *Please*."

There was a murmur of voices outside the alcove and one of the Speaker's aides came in. He crouched between her and Breese. "Crissinger and Ash are out in the hall," he said in a whisper. "They'd like to step in and see you a moment."

The Speaker and Breese looked at each other. She nodded to the aide, and then Crissinger of the 13th and Ash of the 41st were joining them at the table, looking like a pair of middle schoolers who'd barged into their mother's bedroom.

Crissinger spoke first. He was seventy or so, a thin, nervous man who cracked his knuckles as he talked. "The press is calling about my honorariums," he said. "First the rag down in Athens that did the original piece on Preston. Now this morning the *Plain Dealer* and *Times-Journal*."

"I'm in the same situation in Dayton," Ash said. He was in his forties, squat and short, with a somber face and a crew cut. "The *Post* wants comments. The *Daily News* wants an interview."

"Don't give anything to them," the Speaker said.

"I'm in the middle of a primary campaign," Ash said. "What am I supposed to do?"

"You can only make yourself look bad," she said.

"How do I look now?" Ash said. "These checks we get are a thousand percent legal, but all of a sudden it's like we're criminals. Hoods taking bags of cash in a parking lot."

"The Rs are trembling with joy," Breese said.

Ash shot a vicious stare at him. "Is that what they are?"

"You better believe it."

"You're our number one expert on every subject under the sun, aren't you?" Ash said. "You going to swear on a stack of Bibles that the Rs are trembling with joy?"

"I will if you want me to," Breese said.

"From my angle, he's right," Crissinger said. "I've got a source in Torp's office and she tells me he's going to push for hearings in the Ethics Committee."

"Madame Speaker," Ash said. "Where do we go from here?"

"Leadership is meeting at noon," she said. "We'll see what happens then."

"Preston needs to be dealt with," Ash said. "These reporters need to be chased off."

Crissinger gave the Speaker a soft squeeze on the forearm, and he and Ash left the alcove. A busboy came in, poured two fresh cups of coffee and cleared away the food. Breese eyed her nervously as they sat alone in silence. Then she stood up and stuffed her papers into her satchel.

"We're going to take a hard swing at the son of a bitch," she said. "And we're going to use your money."

"Again?"

"Dip into your aquifer and draw up sixty large."

"You said fifty."

"I said a hard swing. Get sixty."

"That might take a few days."

"We'll knock him out or we won't," she said. "Either way, he's going to know he's been in a fight."

"I'll have to talk to the racetrack owners."

"Whoever. Saturday at the latest."

"I respectfully petition for further discussion."

"Petition denied."

"Sleep on it, Mary Lou."

"I don't sleep anymore," she said. "I thrash around all night on a pile of sweaty sheets."

"Thrash on it, then."

She flashed him a wistful smile and then looked beyond him into the hallway. In the main dining room, the hum of conversation grew louder as the place filled up for breakfast. "I'd pretty much decided to lay off him," she said. "Until he came over to see me this morning. He had the nerve to tell me *I* was vulnerable. Washed-up and out of touch."

"My aquifer has a bottom," Breese said.

She balled up her fist and bopped him hard on the forearm. "Jesus Christ, counselor, *give it up.* Are you going to go to war with me on every little goddam thing I ask you to do?"

"There's a limit to what it can yield."

"*You* are my go-to guy," she said. "You always have been. I don't care who you use—or how. Just get it done—and leave me out of it."

They stood up together. He slid a couple of fingers under her jacket collar and massaged the base of her neck. She closed her eyes and gripped the table with both hands.

"Do you want company tonight?" he said.

"I'm dying for it," she said. "But Cubby will be with me in the suite. He's driving up for the realtors' dinner."

"Dear Cubby. How in the world is he doing? Better, I hope."

She opened her eyes. "Call me after he's asleep," she said. "Around eleven. You can kiss me goodnight on the phone."

The Speaker walked to the foyer at the front of the restaurant and, with two aides, rode the elevator to her office on the fourteenth floor. Breese slipped back into the freight elevator, went to the ground level, and left the building through the same rear door he had come in.

3

Seven miles northwest of the Statehouse, in a complex of starter homes fastened to the backside of a mall, Breese drove slowly past 1770 Saturn Lane.

Next door at 1774, a Saturday morning garage sale was unfolding in the front yard and driveway, and the narrow street brimmed with vehicles and pedestrians. He parked his Chrysler Imperial a block away, on Neptune, pulled a black briefcase out of the trunk, and walked back. A few moments later he was inside 1770, chawing a bagel at Lindy Trego's kitchen table, announcing the unexpected change in the plan. And as her surprise turned to amusement, then fear, and finally to anger, he fell in love with her face one more time, entranced yet again by the helmet of thick black hair, the mournful green eyes, the lips that always seemed to beckon you inside of her for more.

"What's going on, Evan?"

"You'll be fine," Breese said. "I would never send you anywhere that isn't *completely* safe."

"Instead of driving two miles round trip, I drive a hundred and forty. That's a substantive change. Not a technical one."

"You're right."

"And you're laying it on me *now.* I'll have to leave in an hour."

"I've got no choice," he said.

"*You*— no choice? Who are we dealing with—Mafia, CIA?"

"My logistics have been a nightmare."

She went into the TV room and talked back to him through the doorway as she tidied up. "So have mine. The girls get back from their Dad's at four. I need to shop, clean house, feed my brother's cats. I thought I'd be able to do your thing in a jiffy, and now it's an hour and twenty minutes up, same thing home. Plus however long it takes the stooge to hit on me because he figures I've *got* to be some kind of slut, or I wouldn't be dropping a load of cash at Wendy's in Mansfield in the first place. Jesus, I should throw you out of here."

"Don't do that."

She came into the kitchen and laid a pile of dishes in the sink. "Make you drive up there yourself," she said.

"You're scaring me," Breese said. "I need you to get this done."

"I like that idea," she said. "It'll be payback for the time you sent me to Toledo to meet the perv from the mayor's office."

"I regret that episode deeply."

"Completely safe? I damn near needed the National Guard to get out of that place without being raped."

"You want to back out of this operation?" Breese said.

"Maybe."

"Come up with a better reason than that."

"Here's one—you're being a prick to me."

"Lordy, that's harsh," he said. "Would you like to strike that from the record?"

"Can't you just say: 'The money is here. Come get it if you want.'"

Breese opened his briefcase, counted out ten one hundred dollar bills, and laid them out like a fan on a sunflower placemat. "Here's half your fee upfront."

She scooped up the bills and stuffed them into the front pocket of her jeans. "I'll need an extra large on the back end, too."

"I'm not sure I have one."

"Find one," she said. "The deal was I drive *two* miles and make the drop for two large. If I have to drive a hundred and forty, I need three."

"You might have to wait a bit for it."

She came across the kitchen from the sink, stood behind his chair, reached around and fondled the chest hairs at the top of his white dress shirt. "You're stressed," she said. "Uptight and rattled. I can always tell. What's happening?"

"Nothing's happening."

"Does this drop have something to do with Jack Preston?"

"Why would you say that?"

"Just a hunch," she said. "There's so many stories about what she does to people she doesn't like."

"Never mind."

"Come on pal, give me some credit. You told me the day you hired me you dug my brain."

"And your mouth-watering ass," he said. He reached behind the chair and ran his hand up her calf and hamstring until she swatted it away.

"Is she going after the guy for *daring* to talk about honorariums?"

"No."

"I understand he blew the whistle on a really sweet deal for a lot of people," she said. "But he's an endorsed incumbent. A member of her own caucus. I mean Jesus."

"Please honey—never mind."

She swung open the sliding glass door to the back patio and went outside. Chatter and clatter from the garage sale wafted in with the crisp breeze. She came back in with a crateful of plastic toys. "You *might* have this urgent need to move sixty large three weeks before the primary," she said. "You *might* be trying to take someone out. And that someone *might* be Jack Preston. Fair enough?"

"I could do without Preston," Breese said. "I'll admit that much."

"But there are ten other guys in the caucus you could do without, too."

"More like twenty."

"It's not exactly one big happy family anymore, is it?"

"It never was," Breese said. "But now we're descending into chaos. We've got gang warfare going on—and Torp has five million dollars to throw at us."

"It's ludicrous," Trego said. "All of a sudden this huge stink about honorariums. The first project you gave me way back when was setting up a breakfast for Mary Lou and five clients. They each brought a check for her and I stacked them up like pancakes, right next to her sausage and eggs."

Breese's eyes twinkled at the memory. "She was scared of it," he said. "It took me a year to convince her the whole set-up was legal."

"So are you and her and me going to get dragged into this?"

"Is there anything to get dragged *into?*"

"You bet there is," Trego said.

"Show it to me."

"This isn't about campaign contributions," Trego said. "It's about *personally* enriching lawmakers. A discreet way for a high-powered gun to pass a chairman eight, ten, twelve large a year to spend however he wants. And *nobody* ever finds out."

"Why haven't the major league reporters exposed it?" Breese said.

"They're co-opted by the system," Trego said. "They've got a stake in the status quo and they don't want to embarrass the powers that be."

Breese nodded his head. "But now they have to take down the head honcho to make up for the shame of being asleep at the switch all these years. Is that it?"

"Bingo, boss."

"The shame of getting scooped out of their tidy whites by this girl from the sticks who sought out Preston."

"The *Citizen* wants to trace the honorarium hustle straight up to the top of the food chain," Trego said. "If they can show it started with her—and us—it would be like driving a stake through the heart of the beast."

"And Jack Preston is upfront with his blazing torch, showing them the way."

"You want to hear something bizarre?" she said. "I actually know Preston a little bit."

"How?"

"Fitness Central—above the Capital Club," Trego said. "A lot of Statehouse people work out there over lunch."

"Getting a break from your God awful desk job?"

"It's not so awful," Trego said. "I monitor legislation—track, analyze, decipher. Translate it into language people can understand."

"I can't see you planted at a computer screen all day, eyeballing bills."

"In at seven, out at four," Trego said. "No nights, no weekends. I'm doing it for my girls."

"And when they get old enough to take care of themselves, you'll want to be back in the action."

"There you go again," Trego said. "Switching the topic of conversation."

"I am?"

"So I've seen Preston in the gym, running treadmill, lifting weights. I'm sort of talking to him."

"He avoids me," Breese said. "I'm the personification of everything he despises. Or claims to."

"He's not the most gregarious guy on the planet," Trego said. "Reminds me of a hermit crab. I'd like to draw him out of his shell."

Breese looked at his watch and stood up from the table. "Sweetheart, let's get moving," he said.

They went upstairs to her bedroom, where all the window shades were drawn. Breese opened his briefcase on the bedspread and laid out a dozen sheaves of hundred dollar bills. "If I didn't have you, I don't know who I'd turn to," he said. "Six partners, twelve clients, two ex-wives, two daughters. Hundreds of so-called friends. And they're all working me for something. I don't trust any of them anymore."

Trego reached over to him and grabbed both of his hands. "Don't let this destroy you," she said. "You're too good of a human being to be destroyed."

He squatted on the back of the bed and pulled her onto his lap. "You and I should have gotten married fifteen years ago."

She stiffened like a board in his meaty forearms. "Don't go there."

"How come we didn't make that happen?"

"There must have been a reason."

"The whole dang ball of wax could have turned out so much better for both of us."

"It's too late."

"I don't know why you say that."

She pried his arms off of her and broke free from his hold. "Go," she said. *"Now."*

His heart sank like a sack of concrete. He picked up his briefcase, went down the stairs and out the front door.

*   *   *

At two o'clock, as he was leaving lunch with the racetrack owners in Delaware County, she called him on his car phone.

"Mission accomplished," she said. "I'm pulling in my driveway."

"How did it go?"

"Smooth as silk."

An hour later, in his office, he was receiving effusive thanks from Deak, who'd called to confirm that he'd taken possession of Breese's offering. He would have to be careful because Deak liked to chat. He was out-of-line to be talking to the man at all.

"I can't thank you enough for your generosity," Deak said. "This is like manna from heaven."

"The Speaker hopes you'll put it to good use," Breese said.

"I didn't know you two went after your own."

"We pick our spots," Breese said.

"Then I guess I should consider this an honor."

Breese thought: *please don't.*

At dusk, he drove to 1770 again. The remains of the garage sale—boxes, tables, racks of clothes—lay scattered in the neighbor's yard. A couple of boys tossing a Frisbee in the street eyed him warily. The side door leading out to Trego's carport was open, and inside he saw two girls lying on the floor in their pajamas, watching *Dr. Quinn, Medicine Woman.* For a moment he thought she might not be there. Then she popped out of the kitchen and came outside to greet him.

He handed her an envelope. "I found that extra large for you," he said.

She kissed him on the cheek, lifted her T shirt and stuck the envelope in the waistband of her jeans.

"May I come in?" he said.

She peered hard at him, then at the girls behind her in the house. "I don't think that's a good idea."

"Sure?"

"Sure."

"This dagblum thing is going to get crazier," Breese said. "I can feel it in my bones. I'm going to need you again."

"Stay in touch," Trego said.

She went inside and shut the door.

4

Representative Robb Zinn, the gentleman from the 97th District, arrived in the Speaker's outer office in the Center shortly after noon on Wednesday, April 20th.

He presented a Kit Kat to the secretary, took some ribbing about recently being named Best Dressed Man in the House, and then turned, as he always did, to lose himself in the giant, multi-splendored map of the state that hung on the wall in the reception area. It seemed like only a few seconds later that the secretary took his arm, pulled him out of the Great Black Swamp, and whisked him into the inner office, where the Speaker stood scrunched up in a corner, behind her massive oak desk, looking out her window at the bulldozers rumbling across the Square.

"It's going to be gorgeous," she said. "I'm proud as punch it's getting done on my watch."

"One hundred million dollars and counting," Zinn said.

"And worth every penny," she said. "We won't have to be embarrassed when we host out-of-state guests anymore. Or shove our committees down in the basement, with cockroaches and clogged-up toilets and exhaust fumes seeping in from the parking garage."

"Every future member of the House will thank you," Zinn said. "It may become your most enduring legacy."

The Speaker turned from the window to face Zinn. She was dressed as expensively as he was—if not more so—and they each took a moment to size up the other's hair, suit, accessories.

"I want to give you a head's up before caucus this afternoon," she said. "We're going to ride Preston a bit. Make sure he's sorry for what he did."

"Yummy."

"Feel free to chime in."

"Count on it."

"Then a short floor session tomorrow, and recess," the Speaker said. "We'll be out seven weeks and reconvene in June."

"Whatever happens with all this crap, I'm going to stand by you."

"I'm going to stand by you, too," the Speaker said. "I want you to know that."

"Without you in my corner, I'm nothing."

She sat down in her desk chair. "The glare of this isn't going to stay on little old Jack Preston much longer."

"These reporters are like tomcats on the prowl," Zinn said.

"If you stay put they screw you," she said. "If you run away, they chase you down and claw you in the ass."

Zinn paced back and forth across the wide mid-section of the room, fingering his gold wristwatch. "Deep down, they resent our power," he said. "We have the ability to make a real difference. And for that they want to obliterate us."

"The public records law lets them roam anywhere they please," she said. "Now they're eyeballing every disclosure statement that's ever been filed in the history of the House."

"We need a disclosure law for these son-of-a-bitch reporters," Zinn said. "Let's find out where *their* money comes from."

"They're gunning for you next on honorariums," she said. "I expect we'll have more blabbing."

"Jealous people who resent me and what I've accomplished," Zinn said. "That's who's blabbing."

"I tend to agree," she said. "Does that mean their stories aren't true?"

"I obey the House rules," Zinn said. "I obey the ethics law."

"Of course you do."

"All the other chairmen are doing the same thing."

"No, they're not."

"Why is everybody pointing the finger at me?"

"Because you rub people the wrong way," she said. "You even rub me the wrong way, as much as I love you."

"I don't give a damn about gracious and polite."

"I learned that thirty years ago. Some kid on the playground called your sister ugly and you threw him off the jungle gym."

"I have this hang-up about nice," Zinn said. "I just can't do it."

"It's not that you *can't*," the Speaker said. "You *won't*. You *choose* not to be nice. Like with Evan's clients."

"Are they bad-mouthing me behind my back again?"

"I'd like you to stop extorting them on the tax reform bill."

"What do you mean by that?"

"They want their tax credits restored and you won't give them a fair hearing."

Zinn grimaced. "You promised not to tell me how to run my committee."

"Except under one circumstance," she said. "When you're fostering injustice."

"I do not *foster* injustice. I fight it."

"If you're not doing your damnedest to be fair to *everybody,* then I'm going to tell you how to run your committee."

"I'm being more than fair. They want special treatment."

"The Limited. Bank One. The racetrack owners. We're hearing complaints from all of them about your tactics."

"They're greedy and overreaching, they're not willing to pay their fair share, and the committee isn't supporting them. It's got nothing to do with my *tactics.*"

"You can't take thousands of dollars of their money and then refuse to give them the time of day until they come up with more."

"I'm doing this for you. For *us.*"

"There's a line and you're crossing it."

Zinn plopped down on a chair and stared at the ceiling. "If they weren't Evan's clients, you wouldn't give a damn about them."

"That's not true and you know it," she said. "Open up the process and let it work."

"It works now."

"Get job creation and real estate investment and the construction credit for the racetracks in front of the committee," she said. "Give them a full airing."

"I'll do that—when the time comes."

"Take testimony, let members vote how they want. That's all I'm asking you to do."

"Giving back those credits would leave a one hundred million dollar hole in the bill," Zinn said. "I need that money to fund my property tax break for seniors."

"Shut up and listen to yourself," she said. "I-me-mine, I-me-mine."

She sifted through the mess on her desk, picked up a ballpoint pen and flipped it at Zinn's face. He swatted it away before it hit him. "Take care of Evan's clients."

"OK," he said. "If that's what you want."

"Find your hundred million somewhere else."

Zinn smoothed back his hair and stared at her with a mischievous smile on his face. "We're going on the road in June," he said. "We'll take it to the streets and let the workers bees testify. See how much they care about Bank One's tax credits."

"I wish you wouldn't do that."

"It will give the reporters something to write about besides honorariums."

"Don't turn them into fundraisers," the Speaker said. "The place to raise money is in your district—or Columbus. Not on the road."

"Let's make believe I go anyway," Zinn said. "Even though I know you don't want me to. Do I have to take Preston with me?"

"He *is* a member of the Ways & Means Committee."

"Unless you throw him off."

"I might," the Speaker said.

Zinn got a dreamy look on his face, savoring the possibility. "Preston is a pain in the ass, but he's not really the problem," he said. "The problem is you and Evan selling out the people with no voice."

"The people with no voice need jobs," she said. "They can't have lives worth living if they don't have jobs."

"I'm not killing off any jobs," Zinn said. "Don't buy that crap Evan is peddling. All I'm doing is picking the pockets of big shareholders and bosses. That's my priority."

"It's not about *your* priority," the Speaker said. "I'm bigger and stronger than you are. It's about *my* priority."

"Evan is in bed with a bunch of scum," Zinn said. "I'm sorry."

"You oversimplify everything."

"The Titan Group despises us and everything we stand for. They always have, and they always will."

"You could learn something from Evan if you gave yourself a chance," she said. "About how not to be such an asshole all the time."

"I'm not doing anything wrong."

"It's the image you're projecting. You're hurting the caucus."

"You sound like Preston now."

To indicate that she was done with him, she stood up, buzzed her secretary and asked her to track down a document. As Zinn left the inner office, he paused in front of the big, framed black-and-white photograph above the Speaker's couch. It was a night shot of RFK at the feverish peak of his presidential run in '68, wending his way on foot through an aroused swell of supporters on some Main Street, somewhere in Middle America. On one side of him was Mary Lou Harkins at age twenty-five—tall, radiant and long-limbed, her hair pulled back in a ponytail. On the other side, holding RFK's arm, was a short, beautiful, swarthy woman, her vibrant eyes focused on the crowd ahead of them, out of camera range.

Zinn folded his arms across his chest and stepped in closer to study the swarthy woman's face in detail. "Mom wouldn't be very proud of me today, would she?"

"She would be utterly thrilled," the Speaker said.

"As badly as I've fucked things up."

"You're not perfect. But you were the light of her life and you've become everything she dreamed you'd be."

"That's a hell of a nice thing to say."

"She was the best friend I ever had," the Speaker said. "Ever *will* have. It's a shame she's not alive to see you now."

"Her dying so young is what drove me into the business," Zinn said. "After that, I had to live for two—her *and* me. If she were alive, I don't think I'd be here."

The Speaker brushed some lint off his coat sleeve and straightened his necktie. "Chin up, Robby. Let's carry on."

5

The fifty-four members of the Democratic caucus assembled at four o'clock in the temporary chamber of the House, on the first floor of the Departments Building, across Front Street from the Center's back entrance.

In a spacious meeting hall appointed with walnut and marble, beneath an ornate ceiling depicting the five states carved from the Northwest Territory, forty-two men and twelve women took their assigned seats. With no Rs present—and no lobbyists, staff, or media—the hum in the space was barely audible, like a sanctuary before a church service.

Preston was among the last to enter the chamber. As he squeezed into the back row, next to the empty visitors and press gallery, he slid past his bench mate Waiters, a rangy black rookie from the 9th District in Cleveland. He swatted Preston playfully on the butt with a rolled-up newspaper.

"Gonna get a whuppin today," Waiters said. "Mary Lou gonna sic her big dogs on you."

"There won't be anything left of me but my glasses."

"Biggest bunch of damn foolishness I've ever seen in my life," Waiters said. "All you are asking us to do is tell the truth."

"A lot of people seem to have a problem with that."

"With so much nonsense going on, how are we going to convince the voters we're *not* crooks?"

"Any way we can," Preston said.

"I'm with you, my man," Waiters said. He smacked Preston with his newspaper again, this time on the shoulder. "Full disclosure of *all* our income. Of everything the hired guns spend on us. Bring the whole ball game out into the open."

"Can you stand up here and say that in front of everyone?"

Waiters looked at his feet, then up the center aisle toward the dais and the big black and silver electronic voting board mounted behind it. "I'd love to," he said. "I'm itching to give these bozos a piece of my mind."

With her cherry wood gavel that looked as big as a war club, the Speaker called the meeting to order. She announced the upcoming recess, dealt with three housekeeping items, and turned the proceedings over to Lynch of the 50th, the second-in-command. In his reedy tenor, Lynch warned against excessive rhetoric, then recognized Braun of the 11th, the majority floor leader.

Braun lifted her frail body upright and stood with the aid of a cane. "I direct my comments to the member from the 53rd District," she said. "The gentleman Mr. Preston. Jack, your interview with the young lady in the *Athens News* did a disservice to all of us in the room today. And to our loyal opposition Mr. Torp and his caucus, and our colleagues in the Senate as well. Your reckless remarks have stained not only your best friends, but the entire General Assembly. You undoubtedly realize that now, I won't belabor the point. But I'll just take a moment to emphasize again to you that grandstanders don't do well here."

"Pontificator!" cried Ebright of the 73rd. "Showboat!"

"Glib, smug, and sarcastic don't cut it," Braun said.

"I am not for sale!" cried Kaminski of the 45th.

"We don't accept the idea that we're all a bunch of bad eggs," Braun said. "'Inherently flawed' is the way you put it. We're not 'pieces of furniture to be moved around at the whim of union bosses and corporate titans.' You looking for furniture, Jack? Go to a garage sale and buy a couch."

The chamber erupted with whooping and loud laughter. Braun sat down and Lynch recognized Ash, across the center aisle from Preston and five rows toward the front. As Ash stood up and turned around to face him, Preston could almost see steam rising off the top of his crew cut.

"Thirteen of us in here have got a primary in two weeks," Ash said.

"Including me," Preston said.

"This shit isn't helping us any."

Preston leaped up. He didn't wait to be recognized by Lynch. "Speak for yourself," he said, much more loudly than he intended.

Eagleson of the 94th said: "Ash is speaking for me."

"Me, too," said Cowgill of the 3rd.

"*My* constituents are with me," Preston said. "They're tired of pay-to-play politics and they've got no problem whatsoever with what I'm trying to do."

Ash sneered at him. "Tired of it, are they? Have you ever had a single complaint about honorariums?"

"Of course I have."

"Oh, listen to the man," Ash said. "*Of course I have.*"

"Actually, I've had several."

"I ask everyone in the room the same question," Ash said. "Have you *ever* had a complaint about honorariums? From *anyone*? Party people, business, unions, good government groups? We never even heard a peep from media until this hit the fan."

No one responded to Ash's question. Standing in the silence, Preston felt his knees going wobbly.

Eagleson got up at the front of the room, cupped his hands to his mouth, and called back to Preston. "Why, Jack? Why this need to tear us down?"

"I'm not tearing anyone down."

"Do you have a grudge against government?"

"I think some people in the General Assembly need to change the way they live," Preston said. "The way they behave."

"Then why run for the House at all? Go work with the googoos at *60 Minutes* or Common Cause or the *Citizen*." There was a ripple of laughter, followed by applause.

"If we want to transform the culture in Columbus, full disclosure is the first step we need to take," Preston said.

Ash stood up again. "Do you want us to report every penny that comes down the pike?"

"Yes."

"Every ballpoint pen we pick up at some trade show?"

"Yes."

"It would be a colossal pain to keep track of all that crap."

"Try harder," Preston said. "Or don't pick up the pen in the first place."

"You're off the deep end, Jack. You've got to be kidding."

"I stand in support of full disclosure," Preston said. "Who's going to stand with me?"

Preston looked at Waiters, expecting him to rise. Waiters swiveled around in his chair and studied the wall. Preston searched the floor for Knisley of the 9th and Treboni of the 12th, and the others who had told him privately that they supported his position. The ones who had praised his courage and integrity and assured him they would be going public with their support very soon.

None of them stood or asked to be recognized. None even looked Preston's way. Instead, it was Hyams of the 17th who stood up, the chair of the Ethics Committee. She was a rep Preston barely knew, a seven-term veteran who was foregoing a re-election bid and leaving the House at the end of the year. She raised her hand toward Lynch as if she wanted to speak. But Lynch ignored her and recognized Zinn.

Zinn had not wanted Preston on Ways & Means. He did not like his inexperience or his independent streak. He'd seethed like a spoiled child when the Speaker ignored his objections, and retaliated by giving Preston the back of his hand at every opportunity. He smoothed back his hair, fiddled a bit with his tie, and pivoted on his heel.

"The truth is we earn this money," Zinn said. "We deserve it."

"Why do we deserve it?"

"Doctors take honorariums," Zinn said. "Ministers, professors, lawyers. Even some of these media get paid to plop down on a podium and bestow their genius on the world. Why shouldn't we?"

"You're not listening to me," Preston said.

"You think Procter & Gamble is going to buy my vote for five hundred bucks?" Zinn said.

"Maybe, maybe not," Preston said. "But you'll listen harder and longer to them than you will to the guy who can't meet your price for breakfast."

"You're insulting me," Zinn said.

"Honorariums distort your judgment."

"They're my lifeblood," Zinn said. "They help me do what I was sent here to do. How am I going to learn the issues if I don't meet people and have an exchange of views?"

"They could come to your office—for free."

"You think *I* need to change?" Zinn said.

"I do."

"Maybe *you* need to change."

There was a murmur of assent from the ranks. A fierce anger arose in Preston, along with a profound sense of violation. "I won't be your whipping boy," he said. "I didn't start this fire, and every one of you knows it."

"You should find another line of work," Zinn said.

"You should re-examine your relationships with some of the corporations in this state."

"Shut up, punk!" Zinn said. The group hissed and booed with a vengeance, drowning out the rest of his tirade. Then he yelled over them: "Come over here and I'll knock you flat on your ass!"

Enraged, Preston slid behind Waiters into the main aisle, and moved up it in the direction of Zinn. He would pummel the prick's face until somebody pried him off. Zinn came out into the aisle to confront him, and they eyed each other with contempt from fifteen yards. At the dais, Lynch pleaded into the microphone for order. With his fists clenched, Preston took a step forward. Before he could go further, he felt long, powerful arms wrapping him up from behind and pinning him in place.

It was Waiters.

"No, no, no," he whispered into Preston's ear. "We cannot have this."

Three largish men encircled Zinn, spoke to him in low voices, and got him calmed down. Preston wiggled out of Waiters' loosening grip and went back to his seat. Stunned by his breakdown in composure, breathing hard from a heavy rush of adrenaline, he sat silently as half a dozen members—including the Speaker—condemned what they'd just witnessed.

After the clamor subsided, Lynch called for a final comment and no one asked to be recognized but Hyams. After a moment of hesitation, Lynch waved her on.

"I commend Mr. Preston for his stand today," she said. "But full disclosure is not enough. We need to take the next step and ban not only honorariums, but everything else we're offered. Our goal must be comprehensive ethics reform."

Roggenkamp of the 43rd grunted. "Barbara, that is total overkill."

"Overreaction is better than no reaction," Hyams said. "If we do nothing we are handing Torp the issue he needs to defeat us in November."

Up in front someone shouted: "The Rs are just as guilty as we are!"

"But they're not in charge," Hyams said. "The time to seize the day is now—before it's too late."

The Speaker huddled briefly with Lynch and Braun, then banged her gavel and adjourned the meeting. Preston stayed in his chair as the members filed up the aisle past him and out the door. None of them spoke to him. Only a few even looked his way.

As he left the empty chamber, Waiters found him on the concourse and smacked him on the chest with his newspaper. "You are an ornery son of a gun," he said.

"Thanks for wrapping me up," Preston said. "You saved me from a heap of trouble."

"I do believe I did."

"Why didn't you stand up with me?" Preston said. "A half hour ago you told me you would."

"I told you I'd *love* to," Waiters said. "Told you I was *itching* to. I didn't say I was *going* to."

"Are you scared like the rest of them?"

"I'm no rebel like you."

"Why not?"

"Can't afford to be a rebel."

"You can't afford *not* to be."

Waiters squeezed Preston hard on the shoulder. "Chill, my man. Calm, cool, and collected. We need you around this place."

6

On April 29th, the Friday before the primary election, the North Coast Democrats hosted a five-county reception at Spiegel Grove, the Rutherford B. Hayes Presidential Center in Fremont.

In the crowded atrium, rimmed by glass cases displaying the White House wardrobe of Lucy Hayes, Barbara Hyams locked eyes with Preston. He was enwrapped in a knot of senior citizens in front of the inaugural gown. An hour later, as the event was winding down, he touched her elbow in the foyer and asked to speak with her privately. She put on her coat, and a few minutes later she was alone with him in the fading afternoon sunshine, strolling through the Rose Garden to Rutherford and Lucy's gravesite at the far end of the grounds.

"I just want to thank you for standing up for me in caucus last week," Preston said.

"How close did you come to punching Zinn in the mouth?"

"You saw me. Way too close."

"Learn to control your temper, Jack. You won't go far in this business if you don't."

"I was out of line and I've apologized," Preston said. "But I won't have Zinn pushing me around."

"He will if you let him," Hyams said.

"Why are you the only one supporting me on this?"

"We don't exactly have fifty-four profiles in courage in our group."

"What are they afraid of?" Preston said.

"Losing financial support from the Speaker."

"Anyone who supports full disclosure gets shut out like I did?"

"That's their thinking," Hyams said.

"What a crock," Preston said. "She's going to help whoever she needs to help to hold the majority."

"I agree with you," Hyams said. "But most of our guys are not in your position. You have the safest D seat in the state outside the urban cores. They're scared."

The spring air was raw. Hyams pulled up her collar and put on a pair of gloves. Preston looked to be hot, almost on the verge of sweating, even though he was wearing only a light jacket over a button-down dress shirt and a pair of brown chinos. She figured he was a few years shy of forty, fifteen years or so younger than she was. But there was an excess of energy in the man that reminded her of a high school jock. One moment she wanted to fawn over him like a mother; the next she wanted to pounce like a panther.

The prudent path was neither of the above. Getting emotionally involved with other members of the caucus was virtually never a good idea. Any attraction of any kind that she felt for Preston was an unwanted complication to be locked away in an airtight compartment in her brain.

"Please tell me," Preston said. "What in the world have I done that's so awful?"

"Nothing terribly huge."

"Then why are they whaling the tar out of me?"

"You're not the first renegade to get the tar whaled out of you," Hyams said. "You won't be the last."

He picked a rock up off the path and threw it high and hard into the treetops. "I've been loyal to her from day one," he said. "Even though she did nothing to help me get elected two years ago."

"Sometimes loyalty isn't enough."

"The notion that I'm some kind of R in disguise is ridiculous."

"Mary Lou is a wounded animal, "Hyams said. "She needs somebody to lash out at."

"I'm an easy target, am I?"

"At the moment, yes. When we go back in June, it will be someone else."

"Have I got any friends down there *at all*?" Preston said.

They reached the gravesite, a fenced-in memorial on a wooded knoll. The rough marble marker exuded a quiet dignity. She left Preston in the temporary company of two county recorders and walked up a short hill to the grave of Old Whitey, the president's war horse, a veteran of nineteen Civil War battles. A few minutes later, he joined her. They gazed together at the moss-covered glacial stone in the grass.

"I don't know you very well," Hyams said. "But I'll be your friend."

"God, I appreciate you saying that."

"The caucus needs a fresh face," she said.

"I know it does. We've become a sick, pitiful joke."

"We're beating each other up and if we don't stop it's going to kill us. You might be able to help."

"I'd certainly like to."

"Besides, I'm not running for re-election," Hyams said. "She can't punish me for being your friend."

"Do you know *her* well?"

"We came into the House together in January of '81, the only two female rookies," Hyams said. "Ate yogurt and bran muffins in the cafeteria an hour before we were sworn in."

"I had no idea," Preston said. "Were you close?"

"Very. We shared a tiny place in German Village for two years. I slept on a cot in the dining room."

"If those walls could talk, a lot of ears would perk up."

"The main subject was men, not politics," Hyams said. "Our marriages were imploding. We picked each other's brains about how to hold on to our husbands."

"What happened after that?"

"She rose into Vern's inner circle, and I didn't," Hyams said. "She stayed married, and I didn't. When Vern died, she ran to replace him and I wouldn't support her. I backed Lynch."

"Why?"

"He was the lesser of two evils," Hyams said. "Her vicious steak, her paranoia. Flying off the handle at the slightest provocation. I couldn't see a Speaker like that."

"Did she take revenge on you?"

"With relish," Hyams said. "The morning after she won, she took the chairmanship of Ways & Means away from me and gave it to Zinn."

"Talk about promoting young and dumb."

"It was the most humiliating experience of my life," Hyams said. "She threw me Ethics as a bone. That's where I've been for five years, hearing bills that always get buried, listening to professors explain how government would work in a perfect world with no human beings around to screw things up."

Preston peered at her in admiration, as if he might be discovering a deep and glorious font of wisdom. "What's going to happen when we go back in June?" he said.

"I wish I knew."

"Is she going to sit up there on her throne, with Breese and Zinn cooing in her ear, pretending all is well in Wonderland?"

"She might," Hyams said. "Or she could throw her weight behind ethics reform."

"Ban honorariums outright?"

"Along with everything else we can get from lobbyists—trips, gifts, entertainment, meals. Clean up the mess once and for all."

"Do you take honorariums?" Preston said.

"I've never accepted one—or asked for one—in fourteen years," Hyams said. "The idea of paying a toll for the privilege of conversing with an officeholder makes me queasy."

"I'm giving all of mine back," Preston said.

"That's your call."

"I've been behind the curve on this," Preston said. "I don't want anything to do with them anymore."

"But let me warn you—giving them back won't make you any new friends."

As they returned to the front of the grounds, the last attendees were heading to the parking lot. The lights inside the building glowed in the dusk. They went into the foyer and talked for a few more minutes as staff cleared away food and folded up tables and chairs.

"I have one more thing to tell you," Preston said. "If you can keep it to yourself."

"Of course."

"Someone is pouring late money into Deak's campaign."

"Are you sure about that?"

"He's been hibernating for six months," Preston said. "Now all of a sudden he's running spots ten times a night, robo-calling every D in Erie and Ottawa counties, plastering yard signs up and down Route 2."

"He's saving his stash for the end of the campaign," Hyams said. "Everybody does that."

"He doesn't have a stash. At least he didn't until two weeks ago."

"I think you're off base," Hyams said.

Preston shook his head at her. "Somebody is bankrolling him," he said. "And I smell Mary Lou Harkins all over it."

"Now you're bothering me," Hyams said.

"I know I irritate people," Preston said "But who really gives enough of a damn about me to funnel money to Deak? Her—that's who."

"Do you have a shred of evidence to back up what you're saying?"

"No," Preston said. "But who else would it be?"

"She doesn't target sitting members of her own caucus."

"How do you know that?"

"She does nasty things. Nothing *that* nasty."

"Come on, friend," Preston said. "Five minutes ago you're telling me she's vicious and paranoid. Now you say she couldn't possibly be behind this."

Preston walked Hyams to her car, and as they lingered in the chilly darkness, she sensed a desire in herself to keep talking. "Did you know what you were getting into when you went after this job?" she said.

"I *thought* I did," Preston said.

"Why did you run?"

"To change the tax system and make it fairer for small businesses and wage earners," Preston said. "And now that I've discovered how secretive the process is, I want to open it up so the world can see it."

"Both worthy goals," Hyams said. "Both require time. Do you want a long term career in politics?"

"I'm not sure yet."

"Or do you want to rabble rouse and flame out after a couple of terms and go back to running your coffee shop?"

"Whatever I *want*, that seems to be where I'm headed."

"You can change that," Hyams said.

"How?"

"Don't be a show horse," Hyams said. "Be a war horse, like Old Whitey back up the hill."

"Join the Army and put on my battle gear?"

"If you insist on putting it that way—yes. Just stop flying solo. This is a team sport."

"How can I help?"

"I'm having my ethics reform bill drafted right now," Hyams said. "Give back your honorariums and grab one more moment in the spotlight. Then join me as a co-sponsor. I need you on board."

He leaned against the side of her car and crossed his arms in front of his chest. "OK," he said. "I'm signing on."

She couldn't resist any longer. That airtight compartment in her brain was not completely sealed. She grabbed his hand, stood up on her toes, and gave him a kiss on the cheek.

"Go kick Deak's butt," she said. "I'll see you in June."

7

On the morning after the primary election, in the enclave of Shawnee Heights in the hills above the Chillicothe Country Club, the Speaker planted annuals in the vegetable garden behind her house. Dressed in jeans, work boots and a denim jacket, she dug steadily with a shovel, laying down carrots, heirloom tomatoes, and bell peppers under the mule-gray sky.

Shortly before noon, a burgundy Chrysler Imperial turned off Tomahawk Trail at the front of the house—a six-bedroom, log-style lodge built on three levels. The huge sedan rolled into a space behind the four-car garage, next to the kitchen door and hidden from the street. Breese stepped out. He looked into the stretch of windows along the backside deck before he spotted the Speaker at work a hundred yards down a soft sloping hill, at the edge of the four-acre spread.

He called out to her. She waved the shovel in the air, stabbed it into the dirt, and started up the slope toward the house.

As Breese watched her approach, he was amused by the sudden impulse he felt to climb back into his Imperial, gun the engine, and drive as far away as he could from this time and place, from her, and the conversation they were about to have. He visualized Big Sur, Hudson Bay, the Everglades. They had been allies for fifteen years and lovers for four, and the relationship had not mellowed with age. He was optimistic by nature but he was beginning to realize that he might not survive the current troubles with his career and health intact. His fate was utterly entwined with hers. And the reporters seemed so hungry to destroy. Nothing appealed to him more at the moment than cashing out, packing his car, and heading off into the sunset. If the deeds he'd committed were so heinous, let the law give chase and haul his rear end home.

The reverie dissolved as she rattled up the stairs to the deck, yanked off her boots, and took him inside to the sprawling great room that dominated the middle level of the house.

"I hate to say I told you so," Breese said. "But I will."

"You going to give me ten minutes to clean up before you harangue my ass?"

"I just threw sixty large down a rat hole at your command," Breese said. "I'm going to harangue you *now*."

"Preston goes in convinced he'll get eighty percent of the vote and he gets fifty-nine," she said. "That muddied up his Earth shoes, don't you think? Bent up his silly little hippie glasses?"

"What's that worth to you, sweetheart?"

She turned away from Breese, picked up the TV remote, and began to channel surf on the muted, wide-screen unit across the room. "I'm sorry, counselor," she said. "Is that what you want me to say?"

"Just once."

"I fucked up."

"Yes, you did."

"I never wanted this job," she said. "I know I'm not up to the task."

"What have you been doing the last four years?"

"I just didn't want Lynch to have it," she said. "He's less up to the task than I am. And if Vern had never stepped onto that Lear jet and plowed into the side of a mountain, we wouldn't be in this situation."

"Let's go back in June and honor Vern by doing the people's work," Breese said. "Stop sweating honorariums day and night."

"I have to sweat it, counselor. So do you. The press is not going to let go of this."

"Tax reform is doable by the end of the year."

"Not if this crap keeps up."

"The package is too full of gold to end up in the dumpster in December. But we've got to get Robby off his butt."

"Barbara is introducing her ethics bill tomorrow," she said. "She's loading it up with every thing under the sun."

"We'll bury Barbara's ethics bill."

"The reporters already have a nickname for it—CLEAN." She picked up a copy of the *Citizen* from an end table and read off the front page. "The Comprehensive Lobbyists, Ethics and Notification Act."

"We'll lug CLEAN over to the basement of the Statehouse and drop it down the sewers they're digging up."

"Give Jack a dunking while you're at it," she said. "Did you see the clips of him on the Toledo news, giving back his honorariums?"

"I did."

"Shaking his fist at the camera in righteous anger. He's nothing but a fucking grandstander."

"You didn't knock Jack out," Breese said. "Can we get over it?"

The Speaker flung the remote onto the couch and went into the open kitchen to wash her hands. "He called me a piece of furniture," she said.

"He didn't mean *you*."

"Just another career politician. Surrounded by bootlickers, out of touch with the real world."

"Have you seen this girl who interviewed him?"

"No."

"She joined the *Citizen* last week, in the Statehouse bureau," Breese said. "Twenty-five, if not younger. Gorgeous eyes, beautiful lips, stunning body."

"So?"

"His head inflated, his loins heated up, and he said some things he shouldn't have said. That's all it amounts to."

"Stick a man on him," the Speaker said.

"Oh, mother of God. Please don't tell me that."

"Are you talking to Deak?" she said.

"I am," Breese said. "He's a hard guy to ditch."

"Get him to find a discreet, private dick up there. Put a dossier together for me."

"Why?"

"To learn a few things I'm not getting from you."

"There's nothing to learn," Breese said. "Preston is so clean he squeaks. We already know that."

"He's divorced."

"So is everybody else in the world—except you."

"He damn near jumped Robby in front of everybody last month," she said. "Maybe he's jumped someone else."

"Aren't you through with this kind of behavior?"

"And we need a mole in Columbus."

"You've done dossiers on half the caucus."

"Get a hot chick under his skin," she said. "That's the best way to pick up something."

"You've even done Barbara. What did you *ever* find?"

"Do you have somebody you can use on him?"

Breese did not answer her. He picked at a bowl of mints on the kitchen counter, popped two handfuls into his mouth, and washed them down with a swill of Pepsi. "As a matter of fact, I think I do," he said at last. "She sees him at the gym above the Capital Club."

"Perfect."

"They're already acquainted."

"But not too acquainted?"

"So she tells me."

"Double perfect. Roll with it."

"I'm not sure she's game."

"Get her game," she said.

She scooted up the stairs and went into the master bedroom suite, leaving the door open. Breese heard the shower start, then went up to the den on the upper level that she used as an office. It was the only place in the Harkins home where he felt even remotely comfortable. Spread out everywhere were charts, computer printouts, newspaper clippings, books, magazines. On a wall map, she'd circled in red the five House districts out of ninety-nine that looked to be the most critical to maintaining the majority.

Although the two of them had not yet discussed the general election campaign in any detail, it amazed him to see that she had picked the same five he had. On her desk was a hand-scrawled list of other members of the caucus who needed financial help: Crissinger, Barrow, Russell, Savors, Kaminski, McComas. It seemed like *everyone* needed help.

The shower shut off. Breese could hear her moving around in the bedroom. From the den, he talked through the open door. "You asked me to fund Deak and I did," he said. "Now you want me to bird dog Preston, and I will. What about your end of the bargain?"

"What are you talking about?"

"Open up Ways & Means. Move forward on tax reform."

"That's in Robby's hands. Take it up with him."

"Get my clients out of the bill," Breese said. "They've got a few bucks at stake, and they're nervous."

"What are they going to do—switch to Torp?"

"That's *exactly* what they're doing," Breese said. "Everyone is hedging their bets."

"How did he do yesterday?"

"All his candidates won," Breese said. "No surprises."

The Speaker snorted. "Torp may be the biggest prick who ever lived," she said. "But I've got to hand it to him—he's a smooth, well-oiled prick."

Breese walked into the bedroom. Wrapped in a hunter green towel, the Speaker perched on a wooden stool in front of a face mirror, rubbing her eyelids. He sat down on the edge of the king bed.

"Which is exactly why you need to lean on Robby," he said.

"I don't want to talk about this anymore."

She flipped her towel onto the bathroom floor and climbed up a wobbly wooden ladder to an empty loft space above the bedroom. For a big, long-limbed woman, she was amazingly agile. She stood buck naked at the window and raised her arms toward the back yard, the garden, the thick woods beyond.

"What do you see?" Breese said.

"I see a naked woman alone in a great big house, her husband and children gone."

"What else?"

"I see an eye-popping hunk of a gentleman caller walking out of the woods, coming straight at me."

"And now?"

"I see that hunk crawling up the ladder to this loft," she said. "Putting the naked woman on her hands and knees, spreading her legs, and giving her the bone she's crying for. *Exactly* where she needs it."

Breese stripped, pulled a blanket out of a closet, and climbed the ladder to the loft. He spread the blanket out on the carpet, put the Speaker down on her hands and knees, and did *exactly* as he was told.

An hour later, he was showered and dressed and on his way. "I'm going up to Columbus to calm down the Limited folks," he said. "Look for me back here around midnight. I'll sleep in the basement."

"Do peek in and say hello," she said. "I need to know you're safe."

8

On the raucous patio of the Red Door Tavern in Columbus, wedged between a softball team toasting a win and a gang of tween girls giddy over the end of the school year, Preston watched Jana Jacoby scamper toward him through the early evening downpour.

She shielded herself as best she could with a ratty umbrella, but as she crossed the parking lot to the big, overhead awning she was pelted by rain. They went inside, got a booth in the back room, and ordered bottles of Rolling Rock. The bartender brought two large cloth napkins for Jacoby to use as towels, and as she shook out her honey blonde hair and dried herself off, Preston was seized by the frightful notion that talking to her again could prove to be a huge mistake.

They might be sighted together by someone from the State-house and stir up gossip and suspicion. He could say too much to her, like he had the first time, and stoke the ire of the Speaker. Or he might simply drink too much, stare too lewdly, and make an ass out of himself in front of the most alluring female he'd encountered in the five years since the dissolution of his marriage.

All of those concerns were outweighed by the urge he felt to punch hard and fast at Zinn's pretty face. From what he had been hearing during recess, few others—if any—seemed up to the task. If that was going to be the case, he would step up himself. Maybe others would follow, maybe not. What the others did hardly mattered to him anymore. Zinn's threat in caucus to knock him flat on his ass had been vile, degrading, repugnant. He was an arrogant creep of the tallest order who needed to be slapped down.

Seven weeks to reflect on the situation had only hardened his resolve. Retaliation was the order of the day. It needed to happen soon—and under the deepest possible cover. He would not leave a trace of himself anywhere along the way.

"Congratulations on your new position," Preston said. "The *Athens News* to the *Citizen* is a big leap."

"It's been an insane couple of months," Jacoby said. "I'm settled in now."

"The veteran reporters must be giving you a hard time."

"As a matter of fact they are," she said. "It's like I can't even write my own name."

"I doubt they know what to make of you," Preston said. "Aren't you even a little bit scared?'

"Of what?"

"You're going after powerful people."

"So are you."

"But I'm bigger than you are," Preston said. "And you're so young I'm not sure you know you're *supposed* to be scared."

Jacoby giggled softly and shook her head. "All you guys."

"All you guys what?"

"Always trying to protect me, guide me, warn me." She took a long swig of her Rock. "I must give off damsel in distress vibes because I get this routine every day of the week."

"Distress isn't the word I'd use."

"Are we getting together tonight to talk about me?"

"No."

"Are you going to tell me your story about Zinn or not?"

"I'm leaning hard in that direction," Preston said. "You didn't burn me the first time we talked."

"So why would I burn you now?" Jacoby said. "I owe you big time. I was a reporter from nowheresville and you took me seriously. Gave me a dynamite interview and a fantastic career boost."

"As much grief as it's causing me, I don't regret it."

"It's ancient history anyway," Jacoby said. "I'm with the *Citizen* now and we're looking at Zinn."

"About time somebody did."

"We can't look if nobody talks."

"I'm ready."

Jacoby rolled up her sleeves and opened up a notebook. "There was an event in your district last year," she said. "At Ida Rupp Public Library. In Port Clinton."

"This is an off-the-record conversation," Preston said.

"Completely?"

"Don't play dumb. We made an agreement."

"Which is?"

"I am *totally* off the record," Preston said. "I give you a lead to pursue. You give me a lead."

"Can we discuss that for a minute?"

"If any part of this blows back on me in any way, shape or form, I'll make your life miserable."

"Whoa." Jacoby dropped her notebook in her purse, stood up and grabbed her umbrella off the coat rack. "I don't like the tone of that comment *at all*," she said. "Maybe we should call it an evening."

"I'm sorry. I don't mean it that way."

"How do you mean it?"

"I cannot be identified as a source," Preston said.

"You won't be."

"And nothing I say can show up in print," Preston said. "I will not be out front on this."

"You're not fearless like me?"

"Not anymore," Preston said. "Let some other guy be fearless and get smacked in the nose all day long."

Jacoby hung her umbrella on the coat rack and sat back down in the booth. "Off-the-record then," she said. "I just want to hear your version of what happened."

"Fair enough," Preston said.

She gave him a penetrating look. "You're not like all these other politicians," she said.

"No?"

"You seem to have a conscience. You care about something other than your own advancement."

"Talking to you is doing nothing to boost my career."

"It's like you're among them, but not of them. And in your heart of hearts you want to take the system down."

"Wrong," Preston said. "I want to expose it for what it is—and change it. And Zinn is one of the things that needs changing."

"This event in Port Clinton."

"I organized it with the chamber of commerce," Preston said. "I asked Zinn to speak."

"That morning he meets you at the library. What happened after that?"

"He asks for his check. I say 'what check?' He says there must be a mix-up. That somebody at the chamber must have dropped the ball because he's supposed to have five hundred dollars waiting for him. He called it his McKinley."

"His what?"

"After the president on the face of a five hundred dollar bill."

"The same president with a statue on the Statehouse lawn?"

Preston nodded. "He said he never went on without his McKinley in hand. I said this is a community forum, civic-minded citizens trying to learn something about the state's fiscal policies. Can you do me a favor and make an exception just this once? He says 'I don't do favors for people who don't do favors for me.'"

"Jesus."

"I'm an elected officeholder just like him," Preston said. "A fellow Democrat, a member of his committee. And he's hitting on me like some Mafia goon, demanding protection money."

"Did you write him a personal check yourself?"

"Yes, I did."

"Because no one at the chamber of commerce would?"

"They said they didn't know anything about Zinn asking for a check."

"You didn't believe them?"

"No," Preston said. "I think Zinn's staff made it known to them that a check was needed, and they buried their heads in the sand. Told them it was in the mail and when crunch time arrived they threw the situation back on me."

"Why did you pay him?"

Preston shrugged his shoulders. "What choice did I have?" he said. "I put the program together. I'm a first-year rep trying to do something constructive and I've got fifty constituents doing a slow burn in this stuffy auditorium, waiting for the chairman of the House Ways & Means Committee to talk about taxes. The jerk actually had the audacity to ask for cash."

"My God."

"He wanted me to dash out to an ATM before we started."

"That is *incredibly* sleazy."

"Giving a speech like that is part of the man's job," Preston said. "Shaking me down for an appearance fee is pitiful."

"Did you call him out on it?"

"Rookie reps don't call out their chairmen," Preston said. "That would be like a cub reporter a year out of J-school calling out her bureau chief."

"Did you tell anybody else?"

"I've said enough."

"Is he pulling this on any other reps?"

Preston gave her the name of Entrekin, a veteran D on Ways & Means who had complained to him several times about being bullied by Zinn. "Now it's your turn," he said. "What do you have on Breese and the Speaker?"

"Breese has been hustling honorarium fees for lawmakers for years," Jacoby said. "He practically invented the practice."

"That's a huge piece of news," Preston said. "It confirms what I've suspected for a long time. Can you prove it?"

"Not yet. Nobody will talk to us on the record."

"Give me something more specific."

"Breese's solo lobbying shop in the late 80's," Jacoby said. "Before he joined Titan Group. That's where this all started — and Mary Lou Harkins was in it up to her neck."

Three tweens bounded past them, en route to the restroom. Preston excused himself and followed them down the narrow corridor. In the men's room, he could hear them through the wall. As he washed his hands and ran them under the automatic blow dryer, their shrieks and giggles had the strange effect of calming his nerves, clarifying his thoughts.

He had said quite enough to Jacoby. He had given her more than she had given him. Nothing good would come from expanding the conversation like last time. The thing to do was go back to the booth, pay his bill, and leave.

He was startled to see she had beaten him to the punch. She was standing at the cashier's station, slipping her wallet into her purse.

"I don't mean to rush out," she said. "But I've got an early day tomorrow."

Out on the patio, they stood together in awkward silence. Preston's mind, body and soul ached in unison at the sheer beauty of the woman. "Rise and shine," he said. "And keep me safe—completely."

"Let's stay in touch," she said. She opened her umbrella and went out into the rain.

*   *   *

Alone in her studio apartment, Jacoby called her bureau chief at his home. She repeated the story Preston had told her about Zinn, and also gave him Entrekin as a possible source.

"Fantastic work," the chief said. "What did you have to give up to him to get this?"

"Not one damn thing," Jacoby said. "Isn't that amazing?"

"Poor Jack Preston," the chief said. "So square, so earnest. Like some slobbering Boy Scout."

"This piece is starting to jell."

"We've got to work the 'McKinley' thing in. It's exquisite."

"We were off-the-record tonight. Deep background only."

"No big deal," the chief said. "I'll figure out a way."

"I wish you wouldn't," Jacoby said. "He could be useful in the future. If we burn him, he'll never talk to us again."

"I'm not sure I agree," the chief said. "I think young Jack is so eager to make his mark he'll talk to anybody, whenever he gets a hankering to. But I'm open to persuasion."

"Let me persuade you then."

"Now?"

"Why wait?" Jacoby said. "Strike while the anvil is hot."

The squawking of young children filled the space between them. "You can't come *here*," the chief said.

"Obviously."

"And we don't want to get a room at this hour, do we?"

"This place is such a dump," Jacoby said. "I'm embarrassed."

"I'll drop by with some killer weed and spruce it up a bit," the chief said. "Give you a chance to strike the anvil. Change my mind about burning Preston."

"Ten o'clock?"

"I'll ring your doorbell. Buzz me in."

9

In the south dining wing of the Capital Club, Hyams left her table and went through the buffet line, and she was startled to see Zinn standing by the desserts, eyeing the lunchtime crowd and crunching hard on a piece of something in his mouth. In the past thirty minutes, she had not spotted him anywhere in the room. He probably had been hiding out in the bar.

He came toward her flashing a nasty scowl. "I'm hearing ugly stories about your ethics bill," he said. "Can I give you some straight talk?"

"I'm busy now," Hyams said.

"Meet me in the lounge in fifteen minutes."

"I have committee at one o'clock."

"I don't talk about people behind their backs," Zinn said. "If I've got something to say, I say it to your face."

His presentation was as immaculate as ever. He was wearing a black Armani two-piece with a maroon power tie, and his bulked-up shoulders looked ready to explode out of his suit coat. His hair was perfect, his cufflinks huge and shiny, his hands and fingernails spotlessly clean.

But the sheen couldn't hide his frightened, fuddled face. He looked like a trapped rat cowering at the back of a cage. She had known Zinn for sixteen years, since the month they'd spent canvassing the eastern suburbs of Cleveland together during Celeste's first run for governor against Rhodes in '78. He'd been an energetic and enormously bright kid, with a chip on his shoulder as big as Alaska. It hadn't shrunk a millimeter since. As she concluded her business and left the south wing, there he sat, waiting for her in the lounge, alone and ignored, picking something off the heel of his expensive black shoe with a tiny silver pocket knife.

The depth of his forlornness made her reluctant to pass by. She sat down across from him on a hardback wooden chair. "Here I am. Say it to my face."

"I don't like your bill."

"Did you expect to like it?"

"Tell me what you're trying to prove."

"Tell me about Ways & Means first," Hyams said. "Are you going to start hearings on tax reform?"

"Tomorrow morning," Zinn said. "Next week we're going on the road. We'll come back in September and vote out a substitute bill. Unless Breese ruins things."

"Ruins things?"

"Tries to take the whole pie for himself," Zinn said. "Hardselling his amendments, bullying my members. If that happens, I'll call a time out and back the whale off."

"You've got the wrong idea about Evan," she said. "He just wants us all to get along. Even you and Preston."

"Who?"

"The guy you threatened to punch out in April."

"I don't know who you're talking about."

The odd thing was, she could see Preston in the flesh, at the precise instant Zinn was attempting to deny his existence. He was thirty yards away, outside the window, running around shirtless on a makeshift basketball court that the gym upstairs had assembled on the concrete roof of the parking garage. Preston and Waiters and some of the younger lobbyists, and in the midst of all the men, the compact, dark-haired woman who had worked as a House aide many years ago. Hyams could never remember her name.

Zinn slipped his knife into his inside coat pocket and flicked some dirt off one of his pant cuffs. "Have you talked to Preston since then?"

"I have."

"Does he regret what he said about me?"

"I think he does, yes."

"Is he sorry for acting like a creep?"

"He seems to be."

"He hasn't said word one to me. *Zip.*"

"Why don't you show some humility and make the first move? You were acting like a creep, too."

"Has he signed on to your bill?"

"He's going to co-sponsor," Hyams said. "I've convinced him it's the way to go."

"I know why *he* cares about this shit," Zinn said. "Why do *you*?"

"I love this institution," Hyams said. "Our reputation has been badly damaged and it needs to be restored. Maybe this will help."

"You're insane to try to do this now."

"That's the conventional wisdom," Hyams said. "I've been told that twenty times."

"Five months before the election."

"The moment is upon us," Hyams said. "Election or no election."

"We'll get with the Rs in the Senate and deep-six your bill," Zinn said. "They hate it as much as we do."

"Not in a million years would the press let that happen."

"You're going to ban honorariums?" Zinn said. "Soliciting and accepting?"

"Completely."

"Lower the reporting thresholds for gifts and meals to twenty-five bucks?"

"If not lower."

"Full disclosure of *all* our income, broken down by source?"

"Yes. And we're going to police it for real."

"What do you want?" Zinn said. "A House full of people like you and Perot?"

"If that's what it takes."

"That's what you're going to get," Zinn said. "A bunch of elitist millionaires who can buy their seats."

"I didn't buy my seat," Hyams said. "I worked my butt off for it."

"Has it occurred to you in your infinite wisdom that some of us might *need* our honorarium fees?"

"Yes, it has."

"I use that money to buy food for my wife and kids. Pay my electric bill and my mortgage."

"You're going to miss the seven or eight grand you've been picking up each year."

"You're damn right I am," Zinn said. "We don't all have trust funds. Servants, swimming pools, summer houses in Michigan. Whatever the hell else you and your tribe have got."

"I'm attempting to have a civil conversation and you're berating me."

Zinn snickered. "You're gung ho for the little people, aren't you?"

"I'll put my record up against anybody's—including yours."

"What do you know about little people? You're the richest member of the House."

"Somebody has to be," Hyams said. "Why don't you let go of your anger?"

"You think I'm angry?"

"I just listened to you trash Evan Breese, Jack Preston, my ethics bill, and my family. Anything else you want to trash before I go?"

"I'm chairman of Ways & Means and you're not."

"I made peace with that long ago."

"Then why do you keep sabotaging every bill I try to pass?"

"*Sabotage?* I'm expressing my opinion."

"Why is your opinion always negative?"

"Because you have no vision," Hyams said. "At least I *tried* to be fair. To put the interests of the state as a whole first."

"What do I do?"

"You yank tax breaks away from businesses with deep pockets and then give them back in exchange for campaign contributions."

"If I'm doing so well for myself selling tax breaks, why do I have to ask the Speaker for help in my race? And why are all the corporate PACs suddenly giving to Torp?"

"Change is in the air," Hyams said.

Zinn's voice rose into a high-pitched whine. "You *talk* a good game," he said. "You want to soak the rich and you *hate* taxpayer handouts to greedy corporations. But my God, you've got yourself some loaded friends up in Shaker Heights, don't you?"

"Calm down," Hyams said. "Don't embarrass yourself again."

"Maybe I should be asking *you* for help," Zinn said. "Because when it gets down to nut cutting time, you're as practical as the rest of us. *More* practical."

Hyams felt her composure starting to break down, and she struggled to block a number of negative thoughts from her head. She stood up and looked down into Zinn's wounded eyes. "Have a good day, Robby."

"Every day I'm above ground is a good day."

"Thanks for saying it to my face."

"The pleasure was all mine."

10

The House Ways & Means Committee met on Thursdays at ten o'clock in Room C-5, on the concourse level of the Departments Building. By the time Lindy Trego arrived for the first hearing on House Bill 66, the windowless, nondescript space was quickly filling to capacity. She picked her way through the crowd that had spilled out into the hallway, looked through the door, and spotted some empty chairs way down in the front row, jammed up next to a bookcase and blackboard along the side wall.

She moved toward them, and as she moved a hand gripped her forearm from behind. She turned around into the moist bulk of Evan. He was breathing hard. The veins on his temples throbbed like small worms.

From his seat behind the rickety rostrum that had been slapped together, Preston looked out over the crowd at the two of them. He didn't appear to be angry or upset—just curious. People in the hallway watched them with keen interest as well, because part of Evan's mystique was his penchant for privacy. He plied his trade in restaurants and bars, behind closed doors in offices, and by phone. As far as Trego knew, in his ten years as a lobbyist, he had never testified on any bill in front of any committee. He showed up two or three times a year to sit silently in the audience and make his presence felt, usually at Ways & Means or Finance or Commerce & Labor. The rest of the time he sent his underlings. So it was rare to see him at all in this forum, rarer still to see him clinging to a woman that many of them knew from her years as an aide in the House and then as his assistant.

More than a few of the people in the hallway knew her quite well.

"Walk away from here," Breese said.

"What the hell—"

Some kind of rasping noise came out of Breese's mouth. "*Move.*"

He followed her out the rear end of the building and down a flight of white steps to a promenade that ran along the slow-footed, muddy river. They stopped under an overhang to shield themselves from the sweltering sun.

"What are you doing here?" Trego said.

"You're not returning my messages so I called your office. They told me you were heading to Ways & Means."

"I'm helping cover the tax reform hearings. There's so much going on this month, we're swamped."

"Just trying to catch up with you," Breese said. "Seems like you're avoiding me."

"What do you mean?"

"You were with Preston yesterday is what I mean."

"For about five minutes."

"Playing *basketball*. Or some such nonsense."

"How do you know that?"

"If you're displaying yourself at high noon to the buffet line at the Capital Club, I'm going to hear about it from *someone* pretty quick."

"We were just goofing around," she said. "It was a spur of the moment pick-up game."

"I wouldn't let you exhibit yourself like that if you belonged to me."

"I don't," Trego said. She turned away from him and watched a passel of children frolicking on a swale of grass across the river. "Did you ask me to get close to him or not?"

"I'm not paying you to suit up in your skants and shoot hoops with a bunch of guys."

"Reading you loud and clear, commander. I won't do it again."

"Just a couple more questions."

"Answer *my* question."

"Yes," Breese said. "I asked you to get close to him."

"And I wasn't overwhelmed with joy, was I?"

"No, you weren't."

"But I'm doing it to help you out."

"You're helping *yourself* out."

"OK, then. Why don't you leave me alone and let me do it?"

"Can you find another way?"

"I volunteered to cover Ways & Means," Trego said. "It will give me something real to talk to him about."

"Why didn't you call me? It's been almost twenty-four hours."

"There was no point."

"I'm paying you to call me ASAP every time you talk to him," Breese said. "That's the point."

"Jesus, Evan. This thing is making you insane."

"Not me—her. What is Preston thinking and what is he going to do next? That's what she wants to know."

"He's going to share that with *me*?"

"Just keep trying," Breese said. "The paranoia is getting so thick in these parts, folks don't even say good morning to me anymore. They just nod like zombies."

"He *did* ask me if I used to work for you."

The rasping noise came out of Breese's mouth again. "What did you tell him?"

"Let go of my arm."

"Tell me *exactly* what you said."

She pushed away from him hard and burst out from under the overhang into the sunlight. "Enough!" she yelled back at him. "He already knows I worked for you. Just like everybody else in this town. He knew the answer before he asked the question. We're running around, sweating our asses off on a basketball court, making small talk."

They went silent for several minutes. Trego watched the traffic rolling across the Broad Street Bridge. She felt anger and remorse for allowing herself to be lured into Evan's world again. The sad truth was that he was right. She *was* doing it for herself.

At her firm she made less than the paralegals and librarians. Child support covered little more than her food bill, and she had given up all her savings to get into a decent house in a safe neighborhood after her divorce. She needed Evan's money to make ends meet. She would take what he offered, do what he asked, and get on with her life.

"The breakfasts we did for Mary Lou were six or seven years ago," Trego said. "*Long time.*"

"The press doesn't give a hoot *when* it happened. Neither do the voters."

"In April you told me this was no big deal."

"It won't be unless you decide to make it one."

"You laughed it off and said it would go away. Were you just bullshitting or what?"

"We've got to make sure it stops at Zinn," Breese said. "It cannot touch her, or me—*or you.*"

"Are you writing Zinn off then? Walking him down the gangplank?"

"That's her decision."

"I'm not the one you have to worry about," Trego said. "Tons of people knew what was going on."

"But none of them can remember all the names like you can," Breese said. He pulled a small envelope out of the inside pocket of his suit coat. She knew it contained cash, probably ten or twenty one hundred dollar bills, and she was chastened by the rush of guilt and relief she felt when he pressed it into her hand.

"You're losing your cool," Trego said. "Showing up here today, corralling me like a heifer in front of the entire universe."

"Please don't be messing with me anymore," Breese said. "When you talk to Preston, let me know. And if *you* start telling *him* the story of *your* life, get the hay away as soon as you can."

"Maybe it's *you* I need to get away from," Trego said.

"Honey, don't say that."

"May I go back to my meeting now?"

"Yes, you may," Breese said. "Thank you ever so much for your attention."

11

On Wednesday morning June 15th, on page one above the fold, the *Citizen* published its first story on Zinn under the headline: '*Ways & Means Chairman Pushes Boundaries of Pay to Play.*' Preston was amazed, given her lowly rank in the bureau, to see Jacoby's name listed with the chief's in the by-line.

His instinct about Entrekin had been correct. Despite the damage he was inflicting on himself, he squealed loud and long on the record, recounting several tales of Zinn's strong-arming roughly similar to his own. Also featured were anonymous accounts of the chairman shaking down two drug company CEOs and the president of a Methodist seminary.

There was no mention of Preston or the chamber of commerce or the incident at the library in Port Clinton; no mention of McKinleys or ATMs or requests to be paid in cash. And he realized that, with the aid and abetment of Jacoby, he had achieved his objective: kicking Zinn in the mouth and keeping his own footprint off the job.

Jacoby was turning numerous heads the next day at the Summit County Court House in Akron, the first of three sites for the committee's tax reform road show. Many people in the room knew her, and nearly all of those who did had read the *Citizen* story, particularly Breese's lackeys and the rest of the guns who had driven up from Columbus for the hearing.

He admired the woman's moxie, showing up in Zinn's domain twenty-four hours after whacking him with a lead pipe like one of Tonya Harding's thugs. He grudgingly admired the chairman's, too. Half of his committee was AWOL, and most of the rest were shooting him looks of disdain. Yet here he was, soldiering on with his aide and secretary on his flanks, pressing flesh with the locals, preening like some holy roller preacher about to ascend to the pulpit.

The ground floor hall in the big limestone cube on South High Street was filled with a boisterous crowd, many of them there to oppose Zinn's plan to apply the sales tax to their businesses: cosmetologists, cab drivers, pet groomers, massage therapists. The power players were out in force as well: Ford, Goodyear, Ohio Edison, American Electric Power. They were attending to assail the elimination of tax breaks for corporations and public utilities. In the open space at the back of the hall, a tiny, gray-haired lady in tennis shoes and a windbreaker had set up a card table to collect signatures for a petition against the bill.

Zinn slammed his gavel, the audience settled in, and as the witnesses droned on Preston could not keep his eyes off Jacoby. She was halfway back in the middle section, embedded in a phalanx of guns. It would be difficult to keep his distance, but he did not want the guns or anyone else connecting the two of them. So he would not make eye contact with her; nor would he speak to her. And when his mind wandered away from testimony, he would gaze not at her but at Lindy Trego, his jock buddy from Fitness Central. She was three rows from the front, observing intently, covering the hearing for several of her firm's clients who wanted to kill the bill's new tax on corporation investment income.

At noon, when they broke for lunch, Trego sought him out in the lobby. "Say Jack, would you rather be working out?"

Preston laughed. "Maybe we can find a treadmill around here."

"I'm taking a walk instead," she said. "Want to join me and grab a bite?"

Preston's guard went up. With eighteen months in public office under his belt, it always did when someone in the business asked for his attention.

But he was not going to put up much resistance. Damn few lunch breaks ever got spoiled by the company of an attractive woman. No tedious policy debate ever suffered much from the presence of a lively, hard-bodied brunette who also happened to know the issues cold. They headed down University Avenue toward South Main Street.

"This bill is turning into a Frankenstein," Trego said. "There are so many amendments floating around I can't keep track of them."

"And those are just the ones we're aware of," Preston said.

"You must know more than I do."

"All I know is, we can hold a hundred hearings and draft a thousand amendments and they won't amount to diddly-squat," Preston said. "This bill is dead."

"I haven't heard a soul say anything that extreme."

"The status quo is going to prevail—again. Isn't that a joy?"

"Because of Zinn?"

"And the mess he's making."

"Do you believe everything in the *Citizen* story?"

"Every inch of it and more."

"It all stinks enough to kill 66?"

"Ten times over," Preston said.

"Why are you so sure of that?"

"We can go through the motions and pretend like it matters," Preston said. "But I wouldn't support 66 now if he put a gun to my head. And I'm far from the only one on the committee who feels that way."

"Come on, Jack. This is about policy. Not personality."

As they approached the entrance to Damon's Grill, two Buick sedans pulled to the curb forty yards ahead of them. Out of the first stepped a load of men. Preston recognized them as Statehouse lobbyists. From the second came Zinn and his aide and secretary. The entire group scampered across the wide sidewalk and through the front door of the restaurant.

"What in the world is going on here?" Trego said.

Preston could hardly believe what he was seeing. "It looks like Zinn might be passing the hat again," he said.

They went into Damon's and waded through the throng in the lobby. Down at the end of a side corridor was what appeared to be a private dining room. Preston followed his instinct and went toward it, and as he and Trego reached the door they met McNulty, Zinn's aide. McNulty had started for two years at full-back for Notre Dame and was as dumb as a door knob. But he was always eager to help his boss out. He planted his giant frame in front of them and gazed vacantly at the floor with his mouth open.

"This is a private event," McNulty said. "Invitation of the chairman only."

"I see other committee members in there," Preston said.

"Yep."

"Can I come in?"

"Nope."

"Why not?"

"Because the chairman says so."

"Let's leave," Trego said.

McNulty slipped a finger in his mouth and drew out a wad of brown crud. "Good idea," he said.

Up the corridor, Zinn emerged from a restroom and came toward them. As he got closer, his face took on a look of such disgust that Preston felt his heart gyrating.

"This gathering is for my friends," Zinn said. He pointed at Preston. "*You* are not my friend."

"Why can't I come in?"

"Because you disrespect me in front of the caucus. Assault my integrity and call me a criminal."

"You're hallucinating," Preston said. "I never called you a criminal."

"You're sure as hell thinking it, though. And you're not enough of a man to step up and apologize for what you *did* say."

"Haven't you got a shred of shame in your body?" Preston said. "The whole world is watching you now."

"They always have been."

"Here you are, in the middle of your committee hearing, col-lecting your McKinleys from all these pitiful hacks."

Behind them, in the dining room, there was a commotion among the twenty or so guests. At the table closest to the door, a group of guns stared at Preston as if he were a scrap of carrion.

"You're disturbing my friends," Zinn said.

"You're killing tax reform."

"Get out of here."

"We've got a decent shot at real change and you're blowing it by walking around with your hand out."

Zinn looked at McNulty. "Show them the door."

"No need for an escort," Trego said. Preston felt the woman's strong grip on his forearm. "We're leaving now."

As they went slowly back up the corridor to the lobby, Preston's breathing got back to normal, and his pulse slowed down. It skied again when he saw Jacoby veer around the corner and come straight at him. It was as if she had trailed him from the courthouse and was lying in wait.

"Representative Preston," she said. "Can I have a moment of your time?"

He couldn't avoid her. He would have to blow by her like a complete jerk—or stop. He pointed toward Zinn's dining room. "That's where you want to be," he said.

"I'd love to hear your take on this morning's testimony."

"You'll find a better story at the end of the hall," Preston said.

"You look upset," Jacoby said. "Is everything all right?"

Preston said nothing, pointed again toward Zinn's room, then moved quickly with Trego through the lobby. Outside, on the sidewalk, they bought brats and pop from a cart vendor and ate on a splintery wooden bench next to a parking lot.

"I can't go back to this meeting," Preston said. "The thought of sitting there all afternoon with that jerk makes me sick."

"Rally, dude," Trego said. "Don't let the guy bother you so much."

"I can't help it. He nauseates me."

"I had a flat tire in the underground parking garage a couple of years ago," Trego said. "Zinn happened to be walking by. He took off his coat and rolled up his sleeves and changed it for me."

"I'm surprised he didn't charge you five hundred bucks."

"He's not a total monster," Trego said. "Beneath that ugly veneer, I really believe there's a decent human being struggling to get out."

"The sad thing is I love his bill," Preston said. "We're taking three hundred million dollars away from corporations and the rich and giving it to wage earners."

"It won't stay like that," Trego said. "Not if my bosses and Titan Group and the rest of the guns have their way."

"And Zinn is more than happy to oblige them—for the right price. Isn't that how they play the game?"

"If the chairman is with you, you almost always get what you want."

"You used to work for Breese," Preston said. "So I guess you know what you're talking about."

"Before he got rich and famous and tight with the Speaker," Trego said. "It was eons ago."

Preston hesitated for a moment before he spoke. "I saw him whisk you away out in front of C-5 last week down in Columbus," he said. "Like he was in urgent need of *something*. That wasn't eons ago." He sensed her uneasiness at the mention of Breese; he could see he'd zinged her hard. He gathered up their trash and stuffed it in a bag. "The engines of government will have to churn on without me this afternoon," he said.

"Where are you going?"

"To take a look at the Rubber Bowl, and the giant hangar where they moor the Goodyear blimp. Would you like to come with me?"

"I've got to keep working," Trego said. "Sometime, though. In Columbus. Let's get together and have a couple of beers."

He grabbed her hand awkwardly. "I'd like that," Preston said. "I'd like that very much."

He jumped off the bench, dumped the trash bag, and headed to his car.

*   *   *

Before the hearing resumed, Trego went down to the basement level of the courthouse and called Breese collect from a pay phone. She told him about the ugly run-in with Zinn and McNulty, the brief encounter with Jacoby, and the fact that Preston had spied them together before the Ways & Means meeting a week before.

"We're connected in his mind," Trego said. "He can't get over the idea that I'm still close to you."

"We can't do much about that."

"And he's crazy, Evan. So crazy I think it's time to call this whole operation off."

"Don't pull out on me."

"I thought he was going to smack Zinn in the mouth right there in the middle of Damon's. I really did."

"You're springing this on me with no warning."

"Jesus, what are you—her slave?"

"Give me my money back."

"No way."

"I need it."

"I need it more than you do," Trego said. "And I'm out. I've filed my last report on Jack Preston."

"Why?"

"Too messy, too ugly, too dangerous," Trego said. "And besides—I think I might be falling in love with the guy."

Breese moaned in anguish.

"My lips are sealed," Trego said. "Don't contact me again."

12

"There's got to be a way out of here," Breese said.

"Where's here?" Hyams said.

"A caucus blowing apart at the seams."

"Where you want to go?"

"Away from all the infighting," Breese said. "Back to the days when we operated from a position of strength. With unity and confidence."

"I don't know if that's possible anymore."

Seated alone with him in the bar of the Capital Club at one o'clock on Friday afternoon, Hyams found it more painful than amusing to hear Breese's cry for help. He did not ask often. As gregarious as he was, it had never been his way to solicit advice. He had not sought her counsel on an issue of any importance in years. After the House adjourned for the week, she'd stayed in town an extra night to visit her son and had been on the way out of her office when his call came through.

She went immediately to his side. Evan Breese was hard to resist. He was not a despot like Mary Lou Harkins, or an ogre like Robby Zinn, or a frisky pup like Jack Preston struggling to pick up the scent. He was a compassionate man who loved the institution as much, if not more, than she did. He also loved lucre, and just about everything it could buy. Despite that weakness, he usually strived to do the right thing, and succeeded a fair amount of the time. Far more frequently than the vast majority of his fellow travelers in the lobbying trade.

In their booth, she nursed a bowl of vegetable soup while he gulped red pop and downed a basket of potato skins.

Breese sighed sadly. "This freak show up in Akron yesterday. Good Lord."

"Was it as sassy as I'm hearing?"

"Apparently so," Breese said. "A couple of our folks were there and saw the whole thing."

"At least it didn't make the papers."

"Not yet," Breese said. "But the *Citizen* is nosing around."

"If I show you the light at the end of the tunnel, can you relay the message to Mary Lou?"

"I can try," Breese said. "But she isn't listening to me real hard at the moment."

"I got a letter from Common Cause this morning," Hyams said. "They're asking the Ethics Committee to investigate Zinn."

"He's not doing anything illegal," Breese said. "Or breaking any House rules."

"He's demanding money for face time," Hyams said. "I happen to think it stinks."

"I know you do," Breese said. "And I love you anyway. But nobody's got much of a beef except you and Preston and Common Cause."

"Akron was the last straw," Hyams said. "The day after the *Citizen* story and he's rubbing his pony-up lunch in our faces. If she doesn't deal with him now, she's going to lose *everybody*."

"Deal with him how?"

"Grant the Common Cause request and investigate him," she said. "Take away his chairmanship until we resolve the issue."

"She won't do that," Breese said.

"Ignoring the situation worked for a couple of months," Hyams said. "But the *Citizen* has forced her hand."

"Why do you care?" Breese said. "You're retiring."

"You know damn well why I care," Hyams said. "This is about the survival of the majority. And I'm not going to sit around picking fuzzies out of my bellybutton just because the rest of you are."

"Ouch."

"I'm going to move on him," Hyams said. "Light a fire under *his* ass—and *yours*—and *hers*."

"I understand he wants an open hearing," Breese said. "Just like the Rs."

"I have no problem with open."

"The law says closed."

"We'll see what the law says," Hyams said. "And we'll see how the committee feels about it. Just tell her to stay out of our way."

"Be careful," Breese said. "She took Ways & Means away from you. She'll take Ethics away if you get out of line."

"In the middle of this? She wouldn't dare," Hyams said. "Besides, there isn't anyone else in the caucus with enough credibility to chair Ethics."

"And if you all decide to put Zinn in the timeout box you will royally muck up his tax reform bill."

"Isn't that what you want?" Hyams said. "Declare the bill dead, tell your clients their tax breaks are safe, and go dig into a juicy steak at Morton's."

"I was hoping to keep the plates twirling a while longer," Breese said. "I'd like to rack up some more billable hours for me and my staff."

"Rack on, good buddy."

"Don't my clients have a right to petition their government for a redress of grievances?"

"Absolutely."

"Can't I make money for myself and my family?" Breese said. "I didn't take a vow of poverty when I signed onto this gig."

"There's another thing you need to tell her," Hyams said. "CLEAN has been stalled for weeks in the Reference Committee. Get her to assign it to Ethics, and let us hold hearings."

"You can't legislate ethical behavior," Breese said.

"We can set the bar higher. We have to raise expectations."

"No matter how tight the law is, there will always be people who exploit loopholes."

"Are you one of them?"

Breese looked into his tumbler of red pop and swirled his ice cubes. "I've play things a bit loose at times," he said softly. "I'm not the most meticulous record keeper to ever come down the pike. But exploiting loopholes? That sounds like something *deliberate*."

"Preston thinks you took a shot at him in his primary," Hyams said.

"He *what*?"

"He thinks you moved money to Deak as payback for outing the honorarium racket in the *Athens News*."

Breese studied the weather map on the TV screen above the bar for a long moment. Then he wiped his hands with a big cloth napkin. "You heard that out of his own mouth?"

Hyams nodded. "And he's convinced Mary Lou is behind it."

"How in hay did he get that idea? She doesn't go after her own."

"That's what I told him," Hyams said.

"He's confusing her with Torp. He's chased three or four guys he didn't like out of his caucus."

"Torp could be running this place next year," Hyams said. "That's why we need to pass the ethics bill now."

"You're swimming upstream."

"Should I just give up then?"

"You'll be shutting down free drinks and meals in Columbus."

"Yep."

"Comp tickets to the high school basketball tournament. Family passes to Cedar Point."

"It's going to be one tough law," Hyams said.

"You don't have a law yet," Breese said. "All you've got is a bill. And if you voted tomorrow you'd have 97 no and two yes— you and Preston."

"If that's all the support I've got, why are you fretting so much?"

"Why are *you*?" Breese said. "You're killing an anthill with an atomic bomb. Can't we seek some middle ground?"

"If we seek middle ground, you'll be raising money for Torp next year," she said. "Won't that be fun?"

Breese let out a wheezy sigh. "Then I'll lure you out of retirement to set up shop with me," he said. "You've always carried weight on both sides of the aisle."

"Thank you."

"It'll beat being the token Democrat at Titan."

"I've got to say you've never been a good fit with the Titan gang," Hyams said. "They don't remind me much of Bravo Company at Khe Sanh."

Breese laughed softly. "To mention those ninnies in the same breath as my brothers at Khe Sanh is an insult." He looked at her wistfully. "We could have used you on the inside the past four years. If you'd been with us, maybe none of this would be happening."

Hyams finished her soup and got ready to leave. As poignant as it might be, there was no point in rehashing what might have been with Breese. "I'm scheduling an Ethics meeting for next Wednesday," she said. "We're going to set the ground rules on Zinn."

"Can you talk to her first?"

"I don't see any reason to."

"Try to hash something out you can both live with?"

"She can shut me down if she wants to."

"She might."

"Not this time," Hyams said. "We're going to make it happen. And there's not a damn thing she can do about it."

13

In the living room of his house on Vineyard Circle in Port Clinton, Preston dozed on the couch after a Sunday of biking and hiking at Crane Creek State Park on Lake Erie.

At five o'clock his phone rang. He lifted himself up and then, shirtless and shoeless in front of the muted TV, he sat listening not to the hoarse whisper of his mother, whose call he had been expecting, but to the velvety baritone of Andrew Torp. The same baritone that had saturated talk radio all spring, praising Newt Gingrich's Contract with America, condemning the decadent lifestyles of Mary Lou Harkins and Bill and Hillary Clinton, and calling on voters to throw the last remaining Democrats out of every public office in the state on November 8th.

"Hello, Jack. Am I catching you in the middle of something?"

That was thoughtful, disarming. Preston couldn't remember any other caller asking him that. "Not at all."

"I humbly request ten minutes of your time. I imagine I've surprised you."

"Totally."

"Have we ever talked?"

There had been a sixty-second conversation back in January, in the lobby of the Center, related to the amount of revenue produced by the state income tax. "No," Preston said. "I don't think we have."

"I've thought about contacting you for a while now," Torp said. "Went round and round and finally figured better to catch you at home, away from prying eyes and ears in Columbus. Are you feeling OK?"

"Yes, I'm fine."

"That's the main reason for my call," Torp said. "To find out how you're coping with these attacks on you."

"Things are looking up," Preston said.

"As one public official to another—*as one human being to another*—I have to tell you I think it's a disgrace. The way she's treating you."

"I'm through the worst of it."

"I realize you're suspicious of my motives," Torp said. "Surprised at getting a call, and angry at me at the same time for cold cocking you like this."

"All of the above—yes."

Trop chortled into his ear. "That's funny, Jack. A lot of folks don't appreciate your deadpan humor but I do."

"Coming from you, that's a heck of a compliment."

"From me?"

"You don't reach across the aisle—for *anything.*"

"What am I doing right now?" Torp said. "People who say I don't reach across the aisle don't know me. They lampoon me as Captain God, Guns, and Glory and think they've got me *all* figured out. It's not about your humor, anyway."

"What is it about?"

"My leadership team thinks the world of you," Torp said. "So does a healthy chunk of my caucus. And the honest-to-God truth is I just want you to know how much we admire what you're doing with CLEAN."

"Can I get any of you interested in signing on?"

"It sounds crazy to say this but you're an outside-the-box kind of guy so I will. Stranger things have happened. O.J. Simpson just murdered his wife, right? So the notion of *us* getting behind *your* ethics bill is not certifiably insane. If CLEAN is what it's going to take to stop the hypocrisy, the erosion of trust, the what's-in-it-for-me mentality that's running government, we'll take a hard look at it."

"We're failing in our mission," Preston said. "We've got to change the culture in Columbus."

"I couldn't agree more."

"We have a covenant with the citizens to govern with honor and integrity."

"And we've broken it," Torp said. "Smashed it to smithcreens."

"Maybe we should stop being so damn *practical*, find out what's *right*, and do it."

"You're getting me excited, Jack."

They were silent for a moment. Preston stood up off the couch and studied the face and cleavage of the newscaster on the TV screen. "How can we jump start tax reform?" he said. "Now that Zinn has stained the process."

"If there's a more toxic man in the world, I haven't met him," Torp said. "What I'm hearing is he takes honorarium checks and doesn't even show up for the events. Can you believe that?"

"I'd believe anything about Zinn."

"The way to jump start tax reform is to get rid of him," Torp said. "But we'll have to wait for the voters of the 97th to do that. It doesn't look like our illustrious Speaker is going to lay a feather on him."

"I'm afraid you're right."

"She's going to stonewall and tell everybody to go jump in a lake."

"Not if Barbara Hyams has anything to say about it."

"Unfortunately, she doesn't," Torp said. "It seems like the blind leading the blind over on your side." He paused and breathed heavily into Preston's ear. "Tell me Jack, have you ever thought about switching parties?"

The shock of the question wobbled his bone-tired legs. Phone in hand, he walked to the refrigerator in the kitchen, pulled out a bottle of Rolling Rock, uncapped it, and took four long swallows. "We're crossing the line now," he said. "You've had a nice little off-the-record chat with the enemy. But this is as far as we're going."

"You're hardly an enemy," Torp said. "I prefer to think of you as a misguided colleague."

"What gave you the idea I'd be willing to switch parties?"

"You're a maverick," Torp said. "You've got no ties to the Democrat establishment. You don't owe them a thing."

"I can't imagine *any* scenario," Preston said. "We have huge philosophical differences."

"America is the mightiest country in the history of the world," Torp said. "Faith and family—not government—are the foundation of a free society. And if you work hard here, you can rise above your origins and achieve the American dream. That's our philosophy."

"It's elegantly simple," Preston said.

"You don't have any *real* problem with it, do you?"

"Yes. But never mind."

He heard Torp grunt and swallow something down his throat. "I don't mean switch *now,*" he said. "Run and win as a D in November first."

"Why are you and everybody else so sure I'm going to win?"

"Because this bozo I'm running against you couldn't get elected if he was the only name on the ballot," Torp said. "Let's see who wins how many seats on November 8th and come back in December and have a cup of coffee. What do you say?"

"I'll take a pass."

"You won't have a cup of coffee with me in the lame duck?"

"What would my constituents think?"

"*Never* would I ask you to do *anything* to hurt your constituents."

"If I switched parties they'd see me as a traitor," Preston said. "They'd throw me out on my ass."

"There might come a time when turning traitor would be the best thing you could possibly do for them."

"I couldn't work with you on a long-term basis," Preston said.

"Don't sell yourself short," Torp said. "You're on the term limits clock like all of us. It'd be a shame to waste the time you *do* have left putzing around in the minority. That's no fun."

Preston finished his beer and pulled another bottle out of the refrigerator. The conversation was starting to unnerve him. He was taking Torp's braggadocio and flattery too seriously and entangling himself in the machinations of a man he not merely disliked, but reviled. The idea of other members of the caucus flirting with Torp in secret revolted him. Yet here he was doing exactly that—and feeling exhilarated.

"I'll let you go," Torp said suddenly, as if sensing his anxiety. "I don't know why you're slamming the door in my face, given the way she's treated you. For crying out loud, there's a rumor around that the woman backed Deak in your primary."

Preston took a long, deep breath and spoke as calmly as he could. "Tell me what you've heard."

"That she took a whack at you, that's all. It's coming from a friend of a friend."

"Does your friend of a friend think Evan Breese had something to do with it?"

"Is the sun going to rise tomorrow morning?"

"Who else?"

"Whenever Breese gets mentioned, the name that comes up is Lindy Trego. Do you happen to know her?"

"Just slightly."

"She started out as an aide with Breese in the House twelve, fifteen years ago. Apparently they were engaged at one point."

"How is she involved?"

"I'm not saying she is," Torp said. "I'm saying she *might* be. At least that's what I'm hearing. But you know how things in our business can snowball."

Preston plopped down on a stool in the middle of the kitchen. "Things snowball because they're true," he said. Somewhere in Torp's space, another phone started ringing.

"In any case, you now have access to the somewhat honorable Minority Leader," Torp said. He gave Preston the number of his private line and hung up.

Preston finished his Rock, then a third and fourth, before he dropped back onto the couch and fell asleep. At dusk, he rallied himself, ate a bowl of pasta and finished off the six-pack and a couple of cans of lager. Around eleven, he felt the need for a nightcap and downed two shots from the bottle of Chopin vodka that he usually reserved for special occasions.

Then he realized that the Chopin was appropriate because the evening *was* a special occasion. He'd made the momentous discovery that, when it came to playing power games at the State-house, he was a toad, being tossed around by a pack of jaguars. And if didn't get his act together and escape quickly, one of them was going to pluck him out of the air with a big meaty claw, chew him up, and swallow him down.

Shortly before dawn, he stumbled off the couch and into the lavatory. He dropped to his knees and retched long and hard into the toilet.

14

Early Wednesday morning, in her inner office at the Center, the Speaker paced behind her desk like a nervous cat, watching the hardhats on the Statehouse lawn arriving for work. Seated around her coffee table were the three other members of the majority leadership team: Lynch, Braun and DeRoberts of the 31st, the floor leader.

Together, making stilted small talk, they awaited the arrival of Zinn. When he had not arrived by 7:40 for the 7:30 meeting, the Speaker went into a silent rage, keeping her face hidden from the others so they would not see the foamy film of spittle crusting on her upper lip. This was classic Robby, giving them all an up yours before he swaggered in to get the bad news. She fancied the thought of ripping his eyeballs out the instant he showed his face.

He arrived thirty seconds later. As Lynch opened the door, she quickly wiped her lip with a tissue, turned around, and met Robby's glare with one of her own.

"Sit down," she said.

"If you don't mind, I'll stand."

DeRoberts rumbled out of his chair, jarring the coffee table. He was six-foot-six, two hundred and sixty pounds, the biggest man in the General Assembly. "We'll stand with you then," he said, glowering at Zinn. "It'll keep things short and sweet."

The Speaker nodded, Braun sprang up off the couch on her cane, and Lynch leaned against the door, cell phone in hand, biting his fingernails.

"We want you to step down as chair of Ways & Means," the Speaker said. "Effective immediately."

"I don't see any reason why I should."

"Until the Ethics Committee hears the complaint against you and the House takes action."

"Entrekin is blabbing the private business of the caucus to the *Citizen*. Why don't you ask him to step down?"

"We're going to make the announcement in two hours," she said.

"And you said you might kick Preston off if I asked. How about today?"

"Don't make us force you out," DeRoberts said. "It will be much better for everyone if you step down on your own."

"You promised to stand by me," Zinn said to the Speaker. "Do the rest of them know that?"

Braun leaned on her cane across the coffee table, closer to Zinn's face. "She stood by you as long as she could. As long as you let her."

"I'm canceling the rest of your road show on 66, too," the Speaker said. "No Middletown on Thursday, no Lima next week."

"We've made all the arrangements," Zinn said. "I've got checks coming in."

"Return them."

"You knew about those meetings two months ago," Zinn said. "Why didn't you stop me then?"

"I trusted you not to turn them into a circus."

"Akron was no circus," Zinn said. "We heard great testimony and once we chased Preston off we had a productive lunch. If any of you care, which I doubt."

"I'm moving Kimball up to chair," the Speaker said.

"Kimball couldn't chair a cage of gerbils."

"You will remain on the committee as a member."

"When can I have my chairmanship back?"

"When—and if—you're exonerated," she said. "Or maybe never."

"You're killing 66," Zinn said.

"Wrong," DeRoberts barked. "*You* are killing 66!"

"It's the biggest rainmaker we have," Zinn said. "Contributions will dry up."

"They already are," Braun said. "Thanks to you."

"Am I the scapegoat now?"

Braun steadied herself on the arm of the couch and pointed her cane across the coffee table at Zinn. "I'm trying to move tickets for next week and all I keep hearing about is you and the problems you're causing."

"You can't move tickets for next week because we don't stand for anything anymore," Zinn said. "We've betrayed every Democratic constituency in the state."

"If *you* get out of the game, they'll come back to us," DeRoberts said.

"And if they do, you'll climb in bed with them cheap, won't you?"

"You're asking for it," DeRoberts said.

"Who is standing up for working men and women?" Zinn said. "That's all I want to know."

Braun cringed. "I resent that," she said. "I've been standing up for them longer than you've been alive."

"Is this *really* about honorariums?" Zinn said.

"It's about your behavior," Braun said. "You're obnoxious and outrageous."

"You've all done it," Zinn said. He waited for a response, and when there was none, he went on. "Every one of you used to make as much money as I do at this—if not more."

"We didn't troll," DeRoberts said. "Offer our wares like a hooker on a street corner."

Zinn looked at DeRoberts. "You're my boss," he said. "If I'm a hooker, what does that make you?"

"You're begging for it," DeRoberts said.

"I have the audacity to demand what I'm worth," Zinn said. "Is that what offends you?"

"Return phone calls," DeRoberts said. "You can't take thousands of dollars from people and not return their calls."

"*You* can. Not me."

"The *Citizen* is going to slam you in the teeth again," Braun said.

"Tell me something I don't know—like who blabbed. Was it Preston?"

The Speaker nodded at Lynch. He came up off the door and slipped his phone into the side pocket of his jacket. "It wasn't Preston," he said. "Jana Jacoby connected with some of the companies who were with you at Damon's. Apollo Tech. Power Maxx. Greentree Industries."

"Ungrateful sons-of-bitches."

"What was your gross?" the Speaker said.

"I took as much out of their hides as I could."

"How much?"

"I don't remember. Ask McNulty."

"McNulty can't count that high," she said.

Zinn stood as erect as a soldier and closed his eyes. "Five tables, doing the legal max of twelve hundred apiece. That's three thousand for my campaign, three for the leadership fund."

"We'll be returning those contributions within forty-eight hours," the Speaker said. "Do the same with yours."

Zinn opened his eyes and looked at her. "Why? I need that money. So do you."

"And honorariums?'

"Each table had a captain who gave me five hundred."

"Return that, too. By the time the *Citizen* slams you, we'll be cleansed of it all."

"All of a sudden this money is dirty because some worm from Apollo Tech blabbed that I was rude to him?"

DeRoberts spun around a chair and into Zinn's face in the middle of the room. "What makes you think you can play hardball with us?"

"You expect me to just lie down and take it?"

"What is the point of resisting?"

"The point is I need the fucking money," Zinn said. "If I wasn't giving up half to you all I'd be in better shape."

"We've got others who need help more than you do," DeRoberts said. "You're going to win."

"I am?"

"You *were* going to win," DeRoberts said. "Before you got nose deep in this garbage."

Lynch shifted uneasily against the wall. "We're spread all over the map," he said. "Spending everything we can at this point, and we can't get an uptick in our poll numbers. *Anywhere.*"

"Step down today," Braun said. "For the good of the cause you claim to believe in."

Zinn stared silently past all of them at the photograph of his mother and the Speaker and RFK mounted behind the couch. Eyeing him warily, the Speaker knew that he was, at that moment, capable of saying anything. It might be a tirade against the power structure, a rant against corporate greed, or something vicious, designed to humiliate her in front of the others. It would be a story from his childhood, when he and his mother and sister lived across the alley from her on Como Avenue in Columbus. Her years on her own, before she married Cubby and moved home to have babies and run for office, had been wild—mounds of marijuana, a string of boisterous men, and radical politics that she'd abandoned long ago with no regrets. If Robby's desire to maim her was strong enough, he might carry on until DeRoberts picked him up and threw him through the window.

But instead of raging, he calmed down. "I surrender," he said softly, his eyes still fixed on his mother. He yanked a tissue out of a box on an end table and waved it in the air. "I'll step down as chairman and return all the money."

A spasm of relief coursed down the Speaker's spine. "Thank you, Robby."

"What comes next?"

Lynch came off the door again. "Go in tomorrow morning and meet with Ethics. We want to wrap up next week. Two sessions, three at the most."

"I want an open hearing," Zinn said.

"You can't have one," Lynch said.

"A closed hearing isn't going to clear the air. It won't give me a chance to fight these charges in any meaningful way."

"The law is crystal clear," Lynch said.

"So I'm locked down with five Ds and three Rs."

"Correct," Lynch said.

"No press, no public, no transcript."

"We've given Barbara authority to hire an independent counsel," Lynch said.

"There won't be any need for another lawyer."

"The committee can dismiss the complaint," Lynch said. "Or—if they find probable cause that a statute has been violated—refer your case to the Franklin County prosecutor."

"What a joke."

"Also, they can recommend one of three options to the full House—reprimand, censure, or expulsion."

"If you expelled everybody who's done what I'm doing, there would be no House."

"That's enough," the Speaker said.

"And up on her high horse sitting in judgment of me is this total fraud," Zinn said. "This limousine liberal from Shaker Heights who's never worked a day in her life."

"We're not going to listen to you bitch all morning," the Speaker said. "Coordinate your announcement with my staff. Stay away from media."

"Why? They're treating me better than you are."

"We are adjourned."

Lynch, Braun and DeRoberts left the office. At the door, Zinn lingered, letting them move ahead, then came back toward the Speaker's desk. "You're not a true believer," Zinn whispered. "You're for the *bosses*."

"Go."

"The guys in the corner offices who sit on their asses all day and do nothing," Zinn said. "Mom told me that before she died."

"You lie!"

"I never believed her," Zinn said. "But now I do. You'll do anything, trample anybody you have to."

The spittle was crusting on her upper lip again. She turned toward the window so that he could not see her face. "I loved your mother," she said.

"Loved her? She was just one more person for you to use up and throw away."

"Go to hell, Robby."

"How in the name of God can you stand there and point the finger at me? After everything you've done?"

"You don't know what you're talking about."

"Yeah, I do," Zinn said. "What goes round comes round." He reached into his pants pocket, tossed a handful of coins onto her desk, and left the office.

15

"Girlfriend, calm the hay down. This is no great shakes."

With the Speaker riding shotgun, Breese powered his Imperial southwest on I-71 toward Cincinnati and a Saturday night dinner-fundraiser with a dozen close friends of the caucus. Their talk had gone amiably enough for an hour, but then he'd raised the painful subject of Zinn, and yet another screwed-up check, and the money-for-nothing situation.

Now, only twenty minutes away from the Mt. Adams Fish House, he was frightened because she looked to be on the verge of an explosion.

"Why in the name of Christ would *you* write Robby a personal check?"

"I write checks to folks all the time," Breese said.

"Why that one?"

"I was covering for a new client who was leery to pony up," Breese said. "Didn't want their name appearing on any list of contributors. I tried to explain there is no list, but they didn't believe me."

"Maybe you should stop doing that."

"I'm *always* under the disclosure limit."

"Why do it at all?"

"*Me* writing a check is not the problem," Breese said. "The problem is *him* never showing up at my dinner and cashing it anyway."

"Has he pulled this crap with anybody else?"

"I imagine so."

"If he didn't show, how did he get your check?"

"He dropped by the office that morning and asked if he could have it early because he was going to the bank. It was lying on my desk and Lindy gave it to him."

"Ah, dear Lindy. The most brilliant woman of our time."

"Leave her out of this."

"What a stupid fucking thing to do."

"It was a perfectly innocent mistake."

"I don't get your attraction to her," she said. "I never have."

"We gave out checks early to other guys and never had a problem," Breese said. "There was no reason in the world to assume Zinn wasn't going to show."

"Lindy Trego has a brain the size of a pea," she said. "She doesn't know who she is or what she wants and she never has."

"That is uncalled for."

"Drive. We're going to be late."

In silence, Breese eased his vehicle through heavy traffic. As they moved beyond the Cross-County Highway and into Deer Park, the Speaker snapped on the radio and punched the scan button, moving to a different station every five or ten seconds. Then, out of the blue, she reached across the pull-down table and poked Breese hard on the cheek with her middle finger. "Why didn't you tell me sooner? It's a bitch of a thing to keep me in the dark about."

"I know. That's why I'm fessing up."

"Five years?"

"After a while I forgot about it."

"It never crossed your mind again?"

"I broke my leg, mama died, and all of a sudden I was getting divorced," Breese said. "Lindy got pregnant with Julie and stopped working."

"'With Julie.' That sounds so intimate. Like she's yours."

"You became Speaker, I joined Titan, and my career went through the roof. Time marches on."

"Is she?"

"Who?'

"Julie."

"Is she what?"

"Yours?"

"No," Breese said. "And I don't need to tell you that."

She poked him in the neck. "It seems there's any number of things you don't need to tell me these days."

"Communication is a two-way street," Breese said. "You got to give it to get it."

"Did you ever discuss it with Robby?"

"A week after the dinner," Breese said. "He claimed he never got the check, never cashed it. A month later, I showed him my cancelled copy with his signature on the back, and he changed his story. He cashed it by accident, he didn't even know who it was from. His wife was sick, his aide quit on him, he was trying to run for Congress. He was so burnt-out, he didn't know where he was or what he was doing half the time."

"I can hear him whining now."

"I've got to admit it sounded halfway plausible," Breese said. "He promised to return the money. But I never got it."

"That's an open and shut case of unlawful compensation," the Speaker said. "Getting paid for work he didn't do."

"A body has got to show up at the table to eat. Absolutely."

"How are we going to ride this out?"

"By pretending it never happened and keeping our mouths shut."

"And her mouth. This creature you're so hung up on."

"Stop obsessing about her."

"If this gets in front of Ethics from *any* kind of credible source, we have a legal duty to refer him to the county prosecutor."

"Understood."

"Then Common Cause and the *Citizen* and Torp will all be screaming at us to expel him."

"That would leave us an inch or two short of dying."

"We *cannot* refer him to the Franklin County prosecutor."

"He'll get crucified."

"We need to move this out of Ethics quickly, with a recommendation to reprimand," she said. "Say Wednesday. Then get it on the floor for a vote and be done with it."

"You're rushing things," Breese said. "Barbara won't like that."

"She will absolutely hate it," the Speaker said. "She wants to meet all summer long, stoke the fires on CLEAN, leak everything juicy to the *Citizen*. But why should I care about Barbara?"

"You need to deal with this and you need her to do it."

"She lied to my face," the Speaker said. "Looked me straight in the eye and said she was supporting me."

"That's not true and you know it."

"Shut up."

"It's a fantasy you've spun so many times in your head you're convinced it's real."

"Then she turned around and supported Lynch."

"She was behind Lynch from the get-go and she was upfront about it," Breese said. "Otherwise you never would have given her the chair of Ethics. Right?"

"I said shut up."

"It's time to bury the hatchet," Breese said.

"Oh, goddamit, *I know that*." She turned off the radio and drummed the passenger side window with her fingers. "Why shouldn't I obsess about her?"

"Barbara?"

"No, knucklehead. The most brilliant woman of our time."

"We're not involved."

"She was with you when you put those breakfasts together for me," the Speaker said. "With you for this splendid little muckup with Robby's check. I call that involved."

"We're not sleeping together."

"What next? Are you going to tell me she's the one you're using on Preston?"

"Actually, she is."

The Speaker gasped. "On the drop for Deak?"

Breese nodded.

"And in Columbus?"

He nodded again.

She gazed out the window for several minutes Outside, traffic slowed to a crawl again. She reached into her tote bag on the floor in front of her and took out a copy of *Jet* magazine and a black plastic film canister. She laid the *Jet* on the pull down table, popped the canister, and tapped a mound of white powder onto the glossy cover.

"Do you really need more of that *now*?" Breese said. "You're being indiscreet."

"Eyes on the road."

"We're in Cincinnati. They bust people here."

"Not white people driving around in Imperials."

"You are out of control."

She pulled a straight razor blade from a red leather clutch purse and chopped the powder deftly into three lines. "I had all I was going to need of this until five minutes ago," she said. "Then I got word from an impeccable source that my boyfriend is fucking his former fiancé."

"I'm going to stop the car. I don't have to put up with this."

"Or maybe she's just going down on you."

"Can't you go to a doctor and get a be-happy pill like everybody else?"

"Because I don't want to be *happy*," she said. "I want to be *buzzed*." She leaned in toward him over the table and snorted a line up each nostril with the nub of a plastic straw.

"It's getting harder and harder to find on a moment's notice," Breese said.

"Why in the name of holy God are you using her on Preston?"

"She's the best available person for the job," Breese said. "As simple as that."

"No wonder you're not getting anything useful."

Breese giggled. "Preston wears briefs."

"Don't mock me."

"I've got definitive proof."

"She's doing both of you, is she? In a threesome? Or maybe you're doing Preston yourself."

"You're disturbed," Breese said. "And you don't hide it as well as you used to. It wells up something fierce and turns you into a mighty unattractive human being."

"Are you fucking her or not?"

"No," Breese said. "I am not."

"Are you sucking each other off?"

"No."

"That makes my day, counselor. Because it's not your job to fuck and suck the little pea brain. Your job is to tape her mouth shut. And your own."

The Speaker quickly snorted up the last line and slipped her kit back into her purse. Breese edged off the freeway and headed toward Pavilion Street and the entrance to the Fish House. A knot of people had assembled at the front door, awaiting their arrival. She twisted in her seat to have a last word with Breese.

"Take care of the car and get inside," she said. "When you get there work the room. You're ten tickets short of quota for Wednesday."

"I'm short?"

"You've been short for a good long time," she said. "Elevate your game. I'm depending on you."

"It's tough to make quota when the whole blessed universe is tumbling down on your head."

"Have the car here ten minutes after we break up," she said. "Crank the A/C and find me some rockabilly."

"Will do."

"Remember the boning you gave me in this machine a couple of years ago?"

"Heavens, yes."

"Do it again, boyfriend. Find an old cemetery somewhere, cut the lights, and stretch me out in the back seat. And don't drink yourself silly tonight because you need to last."

"Yes, ma'am."

The valet approached the vehicle and opened the passenger side door. The Speaker stepped out and greeted the group at the front door. Breese tidied up the front seat, extracted himself, and handed over his keys. He waited until the Speaker and her entourage had entered the restaurant, then followed them inside.

Deep in his neck and left shoulder, he felt a fearsome pain.

16

On the following Tuesday morning, the *Citizen* published its second story on Zinn. Below a headline across page one of the Metro & State section was an account of the lunch at Damon's in Akron twelve days earlier, focusing on the financial arrangements. The sources were three unidentified attendees and the freshly-fired PR hack Zinn had hired to put the event together. Inside the section were two sidebars detailing the collapse of Zinn's tax reform bill and his scheduled appearance that day in front of the Ethics Committee.

In her pajamas, Lindy Trego read the story at the kitchen table on Saturn Lane. The pre-dawn stillness was shattered by the shrill ring of her phone and then the pressing voice of Breese in her ear.

"Good morning, beautiful."

"You scared the hell out of me."

"Excuse me. I figured you'd be up."

"I thought my brother was dead."

"Have you seen the *Citizen?*"

"I'm looking at it right now."

"Lordy, we skated on this," Breese said. "I mean *you* being there, Titan staff and clients being there. You *calling* me from up there. And we all glide through without a mention."

"How long can we keep gliding?"

"One day at a time, sweetheart."

"I said I was through with this," Trego said. "I asked you not to contact me."

"It's been two weeks."

"You're making trouble for both of us."

"Just tell me one thing. Is the press on your butt?"

"Jana Jacoby left voice mails last week," Trego said. "This week, it's the *Beacon* and the *Enquirer*. And people at the office are antsy."

"How antsy?"

"Asking if the revelations are hindering me in my job," she said. "Whispering about me as I come out of the bathroom. Scratching their heads like who the hell is this chick and why did we ever hire her?"

"Would they let you go just because you used to work for me?"

"I'm the mystery woman from Evan Breese's past," Trego said. "That's all anybody seems to care about."

"What we need to do is keep her out of it *entirely*."

"So you can blame me?"

"Those were my clients, my breakfasts, my reports," Breese said. "I put my name on them, not you."

"I just did what you told me to."

"It blows my mind that these vultures are digging them up after all these years." Breese coughed loudly, forcing something out of his windpipe. "You remember that mix-up we had one time with a check I wrote to Zinn?"

"He cashed it when he wasn't supposed to," she said. "And he ended up giving you your money back."

"That's it," Breese said. "Except that he never gave me the money."

If he had been there in the kitchen with her, she might have belted him in the mouth, or smashed a frying pan over his head. "Why did you tell me he did?"

"You thought you screwed up and I wanted to ease your mind."

"Jesus, what can I say? Thanks for your honesty."

"I'm telling you now so you know."

"As long as you're confessing, tell me about April."

"What about it?"

"Stop the charade," she said. "I delivered an illegal campaign contribution to Deak. We committed a crime."

There was a pause, and she listened to his labored breathing. "If it bothered you so much, why did you drive up there?"

"Does she know I'm the one who made the drop for you?"

"She doesn't know there was a drop."

"That I'm the one you stuck on Preston in Columbus?"

"I planned that solo," Breese said.

"Bullshit, Evan. You don't even take a piss unless she tells you to."

"Meet me for coffee when you get downtown."

Upstairs, an alarm clock buzzed and her daughters rolled out of bed. They were due at day care in an hour.

"I've got to go," Trego said.

"Coffee, then?"

"Buzz off."

"It's important we talk."

"Stay away from me."

"I need you," Breese said. "What do *you* need?"

"I'm thinking maybe a lawyer."

"Don't do that."

"I'm hanging up."

*   *   *

At noon, she left her office and went to Fitness Central and Preston was there, pounding a treadmill in a corner of the upstairs room, his face fixed on the cinderblock wall. From a distance, before she approached, she relished the biceps and pecs, the exquisitely cut calves, the quads churning hard under his baggy khaki shorts.

There was more to Jack than his brain. That had been apparent from the outset. Physically, the man was a piece of work, and somewhere beneath that hard exterior she sensed a heart, trying to make a human connection. And to aid in her struggle to take her mind and body off Breese, she was seeking a connection herself.

But why Jack? That was the thing that alarmed her. There were several other men she might have pursued more readily. As involved as she was with Evan, trying to get close to Jack seemed like an act of treachery. To pursue him now, in the wake of her underhanded efforts to hurt him, struck her as a flagrant violation of—what? Trust, decorum, basic human decency?

It boiled down to sexual attraction, and it was a combustible situation. But that wasn't stopping her. In fact, it was spurring her on.

He couldn't stick around, he was on his way to floor session, then to committee and a meeting with the UAW. The girls were at their Dad's for the overnight. She suggested getting together for a beer, and at six o'clock he was waiting for her at Mac's Café, a mile up High Street from the Statehouse, his nose in the *Citizen* at the front end of the bar where she wouldn't have any trouble spotting him. After a couple of Molsons apiece they were in the back room with the dart players, sharing a wooden booth, ordering dinner and having at each other on Mary Lou Harkins, Andrew Torp, and the perilous future of democracy in America.

She could hardly believe her good fortune. She'd pried the hermit crab out of his shell, and here he sat across the table from her on a sultry summer night—alone.

"What's going to happen to Zinn this week?" Trego said.

"I am completely out of the loop on that."

"Come on, Mr. CLEAN. What do you see in your crystal ball?"

"What I want to see is expulsion," Preston said. "But I don't think that's going to happen."

"Will he get Ways & Means back?"

"Even if he does, he's crippled."

"Who's the *Citizen* going after next?"

"Your buddy Breese, I imagine."

"My buddy," she said. "That's hilarious."

"What is he then?"

"You're more my buddy than he is," she said. "If you want to know the truth."

"Were you engaged to him?"

She did not want to answer, but the alcohol was having its way, and he was staring at her expectantly. "I was fresh out of Kent State, working in the clerk's office in the House," she said. "He was thirty-four, the wizard of Ways & Means. He knew more about taxes than anybody on Capitol Square."

"He still does."

"He had a thousand friends, he adored me, he was incredibly fun to be with. I fell hard."

"What happened?"

"I broke it off."

"That must have been anguishing."

"A couple of years later we were both married to other people."

"Why did you end it?"

"Evan had an ex-wife," she said. "And two demanding little girls. He was always working, and he shaded the truth on a regular basis. Far too often for a husband."

"After all that, you went to work for him?"

"I resisted at first," she said. "My husband went ballistic. But he talked both of us into it. He isn't the slickest lobbyist in Columbus for nothing."

Dinner arrived. She got him off Evan and into some insanely funny takes on the more pompous members of the House. By the time he asked the waiter to bring coffee and the check, she was basking in the glow of a sweet, soulful lust. She'd been flying solo sexually for fifteen months; her craving for cock was so urgent that she ached. In her mind's eye, she previewed the second act of the evening in detail: he stripping her naked in his hotel room three blocks east of the Square, she peeling off his T shirt, licking his raised-up nipples, gliding her hands down his six-pack to unzip him and then feel him get gorgeously hard and thick in her hands and mouth.

It wouldn't be a soft, gentle session. Not even close. She had no quarrel with that. Sometime around midnight, she'd surprise him by popping out of bed and pulling on her clothes. By that time she'd have taken in more meat and cum than she'd ever taken from a man in her life. She'd leave him with a deep, wet tongue kiss—to let him get a taste of himself—and be gone.

"Show me the splendors of the Holiday Inn," she said. "I'd love to be alone with you."

He looked at the floor and ceiling and then at the dartboards spread out along the wall. "I'm afraid I'm not up for that," he said.

He might as well have smacked her in the stomach with a crowbar. "I'm having a fantastic time," she said. "I thought the feeling was mutual."

"Taking you back to my room would be a mistake."

"Why?"

"You're too close to Breese," he said. "I'm scared of you."

"There's nothing to be scared of."

"Are you still working for him?"

"No. I told you that."

"When did you stop?"

"Jesus, Jack. Could you knock it off?"

Tears welled in her eyes and started to drip down her cheeks. She did not want to make a scene in front of the crowd. She grabbed her purse and bolted out the back entrance into the lot where she'd parked. As she was unlocking her car, he burst out the back door and came toward her.

"I'm sorry," he said. "I didn't mean to upset you."

"Are we all such horrible human beings?" she said. "Me and Evan and her and Zinn and the rest of us?"

"No."

"If politics is such a cesspool, why are you here?"

"To change things."

"So what the hell are you—perfect?"

He looked at the ground. "No."

"You're damn right you're not," she said. "Always tooting your own horn. Always looking to punch somebody out."

"Please don't hate me for this."

"Goodnight, Jack."

She got into her car and drove home. On Saturn Lanc, her bed felt as dry and wide as the Sahara.

17

Coming in from the fetid summer air through a revolving door, Barbara Hyams crossed the lobby of the Union Plaza to the elevator bank and rode awash in Muzak to the eleventh floor. The door to the Speaker's suite was ajar, and as she tapped on it she could see coffee, yogurt cups and muffins laid out on a table and beyond that, at a big window, the Speaker coughing into a handkerchief and then balling it up and stuffing it into the waistband of her pants beneath her jacket.

There was no turning back now. When Mary Lou had called and suggested breakfast, her first impulse had been to decline the invitation. Tell her to shove breakfast and let the chips fall where they may. But here she was at the Union Plaza, reeling between hope and trepidation, to face whatever might unfold between them. And beyond a frank airing of views on Zinn, she had no idea what that might be.

"Come in, Barbara. I appreciate you coming over."

Enwrapped in the hum of the air conditioner, they sat down in chairs on opposite sides of the coffee table and avoided each other's gaze. The silence between them had been extensive. Since she'd been relieved of her duties as Ways & Means chair, the two of them had exchanged icy pleasantries five or six times, always in the presence of others. The coming conversation would be their first one-on-one talk in almost five years.

Hyams had never been in the suite and she was intrigued by what she saw. The outer room was Spartan and neat as a pin, exactly like the apartment they'd shared thirteen years before. The only adornments were a dozen Appalachian folk art paintings that had hung on the walls in their old place: vividly colored renderings of zoos and carnivals and circus life, drawn with enamel house paint on thick slabs of plywood and Masonite.

The Speaker poured two cups of coffee and handed one to Hyams.

"I'll come right to the point,'" she said. "I'd like Ethics to wrap up hearings on Robby this morning."

"That was the original plan, I know."

"With a recommendation to reprimand."

"But I'd like to change the plan."

"We'll have a floor vote tomorrow before we break for the summer."

"I'd like more time," Hyams said.

"You've gone eight hours," the Speaker said. "Heard from everybody you need to hear from. What's left to do?"

"More allegations are surfacing."

"Tell me."

"He's padding mileage expenses," Hyams said.

"No, he's not. I sign off on those reports myself."

"Taking free rooms from Ferris-Cornell and Wyandot Energy."

"Where?"

"At Loggerhead Cay on Sanibel Island."

"I'm aware of that arrangement," the Speaker said. "Two nights from each of them, two hundred fifty dollars per night. He's under the reporting limit for paid lodging."

"I cannot stomach that point of view anymore," Hyams said.

"I understand it disgusts you. But it isn't a violation."

"He's cashing honorarium checks for events he doesn't attend."

The Speaker's eyes twitched. "Who's saying that?"

"Two law firms in Cincinnati," Hyams said. "He went to their offices, picked up his checks, and left. Blew off their reception and went to Riverfront Stadium to see the Reds."

"There's no substance to those stories."

"They tell me they're willing to make statements for the record."

"Your formal complaints deal with Entrekin and the drug CEOs and the Damon's lunch. He returned all of that money last week."

"All of it?"

"*Every* goddam penny," the Speaker said. "He's been murdered by the *Citizen*, he's lost Ways & Means, and he's going to be reprimanded. That's enough punishment, don't you think?"

"I'm not sure if it is or not," Hyams said.

The Speaker looked her directly into her eyes. "Let's have a committee vote today."

"Are you sure you have the support on the floor for a reprimand?"

"Of course I'm sure."

"The Rs will vote no as a block," Hyams said. "To express their outrage. Five crossovers will defeat you."

"The Rs will be with me. Not against me."

"Why?" Hyams said. "They're against you in committee. They want to drag this out all summer, then expel him and refer him to the prosecutor."

"Torp knows when to call off his hounds," the Speaker said. "If we get any deeper into this, his name will start coming up— and he knows it."

"It's an absolute whitewash," Hyams said. "The worst thing you can do."

"You're going to wallow in rumor and innuendo and kill everybody's chance to get re-elected? That's a hell of thing to have on your conscience."

"It's not on my conscience," Hyams said.

"Torp will be grateful to you for doing his dirty work."

"This is not about Torp."

They ate their food in silence. It had been over a year since Hyams had seen the Speaker's face up close, and she was startled. The skin on her neck and cheeks was pitted and pocked, her lips were horribly chapped, and the eyes were bloodshot and bewildered, the pupils enlarged into grayish holes. It was impossible to put it any other way: Mary Lou Harkins looked like hell.

"I'll throw you off the committee if I have to," the Speaker said. "Appoint Saltzman chair, bring up Cobe to fill the vacancy."

"We're going to meet at ten o'clock to hear testimony. And set a schedule for the summer."

"You're not going to meet during recess. I'll close the Departments Building if I have to."

"Then we'll convene in the cafeteria in the Center," Hyams said. "The reporters will love it."

The Speaker licked her yogurt spoon clean and then, with a snap of the wrist, sent it whistling across the table within inches of Hyam's ear. It pinged off the wall and landed on the floor by the window. "I invite you here as a colleague," she said, her voice throbbing. "As a sister-in-arms. And you're acting like a child."

Hyams stood up and walked to the window. She retrieved the spoon from the carpet, and laid it in the middle of the table. "Me?"

"Rocking the boat on your way out the door because you can," the Speaker said. "Making life miserable for everybody you're leaving behind."

Hyams looked out the window. On the Statehouse lawn, two tall cranes being used to move materials and debris through open light wells dominated the landscape. "Evan told me you were bad off," she said. "I didn't think he meant *this* bad."

The Speaker got out of her chair, went to the kitchenette, and began to buff the counter hard with a hand towel. "If you insist on smacking Robby around, I'm afraid I'm going to have to smack your son around."

"What?"

"Such an angry young man."

Hyams' chest heaved, and her hands began to sweat. "My son's problems are none of your business."

The Speaker let out a long sigh. "Young adults, trying to make their way in the world," she said. "I don't envy them. Especially the ones born to privilege—like yours."

"Yours, too," Hyams said.

The Speaker shook her head and laughed. "There's privilege and there's *privilege*," she said. "My daddy owned a steak house and a bowling alley. Not ten blocks of downtown Cleveland."

"You didn't raise angels."

"No, I didn't. But at least mine aren't slapping their girl-friends around in restaurants."

"Shut up, Mary Lou."

"Stuffing dead squirrels in her mailbox. Chopping up her underpants with a hatchet."

"This is the most despicable thing you've ever done," Hyams said. "What do you think you can do to hurt my son?"

"A washed-up politician like me? Not *terribly* much. But I've still got friends in municipal court here. I'll ask them not to plea bargain the creep down to peanuts because of who his mother is."

Her ravaged face was alive now. The dead, gray eyes had taken on a playful glint. She's enjoying this, Hyams thought. There always had been a streak of unspeakable cruelty in her, and the passage of time had done nothing to abate it. If anything, five years at the pinnacle of power had only made her meaner.

"Take an hour to compose yourself," the Speaker said. "Then call me at the office and let me know whether you're going to have a vote today."

Hyams thought she was going to be sick to her stomach. She stood up and went toward the door of the suite. The Speaker followed and opened it for her.

"You used to be such a loyal soldier," the Speaker said. "What happened to you?"

"You need to ask yourself that question."

"After all we went through together, you betrayed me."

"You're demented," Hyams said. "You know that's not true."

"Lied to my face and voted for Lynch."

With her open palm, Hyams slapped the Speaker quick and hard across the mouth. "You can go straight to hell."

18

Because of the shortened schedule for the last week of June session, the meeting time for Ways & Means had been moved up from Thursday at ten to Wednesday at one, and from his seat on the rostrum in C-5 Preston struggled to focus on a parade of witnesses speaking in support of three D-sponsored bills.

There was Gerrard's proposal to allow a deduction for companies that establish on-site day care centers, Lemon's to exempt bed and breakfasts from the lodging tax, Wheeler's to repeal the wholesale levy on soft drinks. Election year stunts, thrown in the hopper to please contributors or attract media, they had little support and had been placed on the agenda by Kimball to fill the void in business created by the demise of 66, and the clamor surrounding Zinn.

The Speaker had not given him his chairmanship back. Maybe that would happen later. For now he sat at the end of the rostrum, smirking, silent, elegantly coiffed. Most of the shop-worn eyes in the room gravitated to him, and the attention seemed to imbue him with a child-like sense of glee.

Rumors regarding his future grew more fantastic by the hour. He was resigning tomorrow to give his replacement a better shot at holding the seat in November. He was under investigation by a federal grand jury in Cleveland. He was going to come to Jesus in front of the television cameras, weep manly tears, and beg for forgiveness.

Ethics was on for nine o'clock, then off, then on again for eleven. After the five-three party line vote to recommend a reprimand, the word hurtling down Preston's corridor on the twelfth floor was *be prepared*, the Speaker's office was twisting arms hard to get everybody in line. Then just before he left for Ways & Means, his secretary told him *someone* down on ten, she wasn't sure *who*, had seen Barbara Hyams early that morning, stumbling around in the alley behind the Union Plaza with tears gushing down her face.

At four o'clock, Kimball mercifully adjourned the proceedings, and as Preston left C-5 he caught a glimpse of Jacoby out ahead of him, lying in wait again, behind a thick granite pillar. He had not spied her quickly enough to change direction and in a few seconds she was upon him, her beautiful eyes wide open, her mane pulled back in a tight ponytail clasped with a black barrette.

"Greetings, Mr. CLEAN."

Preston blushed. "Why did you all give me that nickname?"

Her eyes flitted around the vibrant concourse. "Because you're the cleanest guy on the Square," he said. "The only rep returning honorarium money—without being asked."

"Maybe we'll have a few more."

"Are you going to the party tonight?"

"I'm a proud member of the caucus," Preston said. "I wouldn't miss it for the world."

"There's a rumor around that you're boycotting," Jacoby said. "To protest the pay-to-play system."

"How does that stuff get started?"

"Do you have a couple of minutes?" She nodded at a man coming up the stairway from the ground floor. "I've got this theory."

"Some other time," Preston said.

"Where are you on Zinn tomorrow?"

"We're voting on Zinn?"

Jacoby smiled lusciously and ran her eyes down the length of his body. "Count on it," she said. "It looks like the fix is in."

She waved to someone far across the floor. Without another word she was gone.

*   *   *

In the 80's, during the heyday of Vern's reign as Speaker, his annual fundraiser at the Aladdin Shrine Temple had attracted well over a thousand members of the lobbying tribe, each paying four hundred dollars for the opportunity to mingle with each other, every House D, and scores of local leaders who journeyed to Columbus to pay homage to the most powerful politician in the state.

On this night, however, less than half that number were assembled, and as Preston circulated through a hall festooned with the flags of 88 counties, he sensed a palpable anxiety in the air. The two giant shoulder-shot photographs that looked out over the group from the stage—one of Vern, the other of Mary Lou Harkins—strived to convey a vision of strength and continuity. Given the current state of affairs in the caucus, that vision seemed woefully optimistic.

That is how Preston described it to Breese and Hyams at an out-of-the-way table at the back of the hall. He'd been startled to come upon the two of them alone together, and leery of approaching. But when they spotted him they stirred like nervous sentries, almost as if they'd been expecting him, and Breese gestured him into an empty seat.

As Preston rambled on, Hyams studied him coolly. If she had been distraught ten hours ago in the alley behind the Union Plaza, there was no sign of it now.

"I have to agree with you, Jack." She waved her hand at the sparse crowd sprinkled across the floor. "I'd say we have our work cut out for us."

"Newt Gingrich is flying into Cleveland Saturday night," Breese said. "He's going to raise a hundred grand for Torp in three hours. That makes me physically ill."

"What can I do to help the cause?" Preston said.

"Finding ten thousand dollars for Mary Lou during recess would be an excellent start," Breese said. "Call it your summer harvest."

"You want *me* to raise money for *her*?"

"That's how we separate the men from the boys in this game," Breese said.

"The fat cats are not exactly blessing me with their largess," Preston said. "I'm in no position to give to the caucus."

Breese swallowed a mouthful of crackers and shook his head. "It is better to give than to receive," he said. "Far better."

"I'm not receiving, either," Preston said. He scooped a cluster of carrots off a vegetable tray and turned to Hyams. "What in the world happened in Ethics today?"

Breese stood up. "I'll let you two talk shop," he said. He gave Preston a quick pat on the shoulder. "Stay in touch, partner. We're on the same side in this thing, you know."

Preston watched him lumber off toward the front of the hall. He was learning to expect the unexpected in Columbus, but the friendly touch from Breese had him bewildered. He'd made it clear to the man several times that he would not support inserting his clients' tax breaks back into the reform bill. Why did Breese persist in trying to get close to him?

He turned back to Hyams and waited for her to respond to his question. When all she did was stare sullenly at the crowd, he leaned in toward her.

"I hear you had two law firms in Cincinnati ready to blow the whistle on Zinn," he said.

"That was yesterday."

"What happened?"

"They got scared off," Hyams said. "When crunch time arrived, they took a hike."

"So you closed the inquiry down and voted."

"Yes, I did."

"I'm surprised you made that choice," Preston said. "It's disappointing."

She cast a withering look at him. "You've got no right to be disappointed in me."

"Were you pressured?"

"Of course."

"Her?"

"Of course her."

"The Senate? All the guns who don't want their names in the paper?"

Hyams slowly nodded her head.

"So the Almighty Lords of Capitol Square have laid down our marching orders."

"Yes, they have."

"And we're proceeding with this ridiculous little wrist slap."

"It's called a reprimand."

"Nobody else gets dragged in from either side," Preston said. "And all is well once more in the Kingdom of Oz."

"You're cynical, Jack."

"You told me to be a team player," Preston said. "Mouth shut, head low, eyes on the prize."

"It's the best way to make a difference."

"But tomorrow being a team player means running with the pack and letting Zinn off the hook."

"If you don't want to run with the pack, don't."

"I haven't heard word one from the Speaker's office on this."

"I'd say she's giving you the cold shoulder."

"And my new job is to raise money for her?"

"I'm not going to tell you to do," Hyams said. "Vote any way you want. Raise money for whoever you please. Torp, Perot, fucking Newt Gingrich. I don't give a shit anymore."

"I'm sorry, Barbara. You've had a bad day."

"You're goddam right I have."

Three lobbyists from the banking industry approached the table. Hyams slapped on a happy face and introduced Preston all around. The Speaker entered the hall and began to work a few selected tables on her way to the stage. Preston excused himself and went out to the lobby to greet a contingent of officials from his district and guide them to their seats.

He ate dinner as quickly as he could. It did not taste particularly good. He said his goodbyes, skipped dessert, and slipped out a side door before the speeches began.

* * *

Just after eleven, the phone rang in his room at the Holiday Inn. He thought it might be bad news from home, or the Speaker's office, and he was surprised to hear Torp's voice at the other end of the line.

"I know it's late, Jack. I hope I didn't wake you."

"As a matter of fact you did. What's on your mind?"

"I'm just wondering how you're voting tomorrow."

"Undecided."

"I've been on the horn all night and I can pledge to you I've got everybody on my side voting no."

"Congratulations."

"Would you like to vote no with us? You and a handful of comrades can fail this thing. Embarrass the tar out of your noble leader."

"Why would I want to do that?"

"Only if it's in your interest, of course. Can I call you back in the morning?"

"No," Preston said. "You'll have to let me surprise you."

"I don't like surprises," Torp said.

"Good night, Andrew. See you on the floor."

* * *

At nine o'clock, the House convened in the Departments Building to reprimand Zinn. In front of a visitors and press gallery filled to capacity, Preston joined Waiters in the back row.

"Let's get this done and be on our way," Waiters said.

"Had enough?"

"Extremely unpleasant situation we have here."

"The Speaker's office sitting on your face?"

"Yes sir," Waiters said. "And they seem to be *enjoying* the exercise immensely."

"This is the biggest sham I've ever seen in my life," Preston said.

"Until the next one," Waiters said.

"What would you do to Zinn if you could?"

"As much trouble as he's causing us, throw him out of here on his ass. Right now."

At the dais, the Speaker raised her cherry wood gavel above her head with both hands. She slammed it onto the thick lectern,

and the House came to order. Minutes after the motion to reprimand was taken up, Preston realized that the session had been
completely scripted in advance by the leadership teams of both
parties. There were no impassioned calls for change, no tirades
or outbursts, just a listless string of choreographed clichés from
each side about avoiding the appearance of impropriety and vio-
lations of the public trust. Zinn, looking fatigued and more down-
cast that usual, slumped in his seat and said nothing at all.

At the moment of the first vote, red lights for *no* appeared on
the voting board next to thirty to forty names. Then the board
was wiped clean and the second and final vote flashed and locked
in. Only two red lights remained. Preston no, Zinn no, 97 yes.

Preston passed through the final minutes of the session in a
daze of chagrin. Had Torp's claim to have his caucus in tow been
a hustle and a con, some fiendish way to mess with his head? Or
had it been real at eleven o'clock last night and crumbled away in
the early morning hours before the vote? In any case here he was
playing the toad again, getting tossed around by jaguars, his name
matched in red with Zinn's, up on the big bright board for all the
world to see.

After adjournment, Waiters shook his hand. "Have a great
summer, Mr. CLEAN," he said.

"I'm happy as hell to be getting out of here for a while."

"And I want to see you back with us for many years to come,"
Waiters said. "So do me a favor."

"What's that?"

"Beware the Honorable Mary Lou Harkins. Don't get *too*
bold with the woman."

19

Raising money was Preston's least favorite part of his job, and he had held only two major fundraisers in the 53rd District, Friday night barbecues in July at the Sandusky Yacht Club on East Water Street. Both had been successful. His supporters arrived by car, boat and bike, his high school sweetheart and her band picked bluegrass on the patio, and after an hour or two, the events felt less like fundraisers and more like gatherings of old friends. Which is exactly the effect he was striving for.

Tonight, his hopes for a three-peat were being soured by the unexpected arrival of Breese in a fat, fancy Chrysler. He had called Preston a few days before, asking if he might make an appearance. Preston said no thanks, he didn't want Statehouse types at his district event, it would be inappropriate. And now lo and behold here the SOB was, out on the dock, sanguine in the summer sun, chatting up Preston's aunt and uncle and a trio of seniors lounging in the stern of a cabin cruiser.

Breese propelled him inside the club, into a dim, stuffy storage alcove between the bar and dining room. "Come on, partner. Aren't you going to take my check?"

"No, I'm not."

"I drove all the way up here."

"After I asked you not to."

"This isn't an honorarium," Breese said. "It's a hundred bucks for your re-election fund."

"I understand that."

"From me to you," Breese said. "Open, transparent, *completely* legal."

"I'd appreciate it if you'd leave."

"Now why should I do that?"

"Because I'd like you to."

"You would."

"Yes."

"Why would you like me to?"

"Because I don't want your name on my finance report," Preston said. "And I don't want my friends to get the impression we do business together."

"Aren't you overreacting?"

"Why are you staying where you're not wanted?"

"Is your reputation going to be destroyed if I visit with your friends for a couple of hours?"

Preston fought back the impulse to haul the tub of lard back to the dock, kick him in the crotch, and knock him ass-backwards into the water. He ordered himself to count to ten before he spoke. And he obeyed. The last thing he wanted at home was an incident like Damon's, a display of foul temper or worse that somebody might witness and talk about all over hell, or even leak to the *Blade* or *News* or *Register*. Jammed in the alcove amidst the high chairs and spare tables he wailed in his heart for the presence of his ex-wife. If she were here at his side to help him through the evening, she would know how to turn away Breese with tact and grace.

"Come in then," Preston said finally. "Enjoy the view, feel free to partake. I just don't want your money."

"I don't feel right taking a freebie," Breese said. "Can't I pony up with everybody else?"

"I'd rather you didn't."

Stacked on an overhead rack was a thick pile of musty magazines. Breese reached up and slipped his check inside the copy on top.

"See where I put that?" he said. "I'll leave it there for you— in escrow. If you decide at the end of the night you *really* don't want it, burn it up and toss it in the lake."

With that, he was out the door to the reception table, slapping on a name badge and heading toward the grills. Preston kept one eye on him as they both worked the crowd. The man was a party crasher and paid no attention to invitations, but other than that there was nothing off-putting about him. In fact, he seemed quite convivial. Far more so that Preston himself could ever be. As the evening waned, Preston found him by himself, inside at the bar, quaffing a beer. He looked to be three sheets to the wind—or four. He had a reputation as a reveler, and Preston could see a quarter century of hard living etched into his face and jowls.

"Tell me, swami," Breese said. "What is the future of tax reform?"

"You tell me," Preston said. "You know more about it than I do."

Breese chuckled to himself. "66 as we know it may be sunk," he said. "But bits and pieces are going to float up to the surface and get rescued."

"By guns in helicopters, right?"

"You haven't been in a lame duck yet," Breese said. "Strange things are going to happen."

"And you're looking for friends on Ways & Means to be ready when they do."

"That's my job," Breese said. "I'm not ashamed of it. No matter how much you and Barbara Hyams think I should be."

"No need to get huffy."

"The thing that never gets mentioned is I work my ass off," Breese said. "It's how I can afford to send my girls to Princeton and Northwestern."

"I guess that's putting Bank One's money to good use."

"Check out my client list sometime."

"I have."

"Are they all giant corporations?"

"Why be friends with me?" Preston said. "That's casting a mighty wide net."

"Do you want Torp running the House next year?"

"I won't raise money for the Speaker."

"That's your choice," Breese said. "But I wish you'd reconsider."

"And I don't want to get any more involved with you, either."

"Can you tell me why?"

"I don't trust you."

"Why not?"

"Because I have this nagging feeling in the pit of my gut that you took a shot at me in the primary."

"What the hay are you talking about?"

"And who's rooting around in my garbage, hassling my ex-wife, tracking down my dissolution decree at the courthouse?"

"We don't take out our own, Jack. The other guys do that. Not us."

Breese swung around on his stool, slid off, and walked up the bar. He got a tumbler of ice water from the bartender, gulped it down and came back to Preston. "Go ahead, partner, do your own thing," he said. "Vote against Zinn's reprimand, give your honorariums back, write the toughest ethics law in the universe. But pay-to-play is going to survive. It's quid pro quo. That's the essence of society, business, politics. Do unto your friends, and your friends will do unto you. That's how it works. You *know* that, don't you?"

Preston didn't answer. He went to the window at the back end of the bar. It was dark now, and across the bay he could see the glowing lights of the brand-new Raptor and the Iron Dragon and the rest of the roller coasters at Cedar Point. He drained his Rolling Rock hard. The dizzying buzz shot straight to his head. By then, Breese had ambled over to join him, out of earshot of the bartender.

"I had no involvement at all with Deak and your primary," Breese said softly. "So what offense have I committed to make you not trust me?"

"The breakfasts you put together at your solo firm," Preston said. "For the Speaker, when she was starting out."

Breese blanched. "That was *way* before your time."

"She was doing the same thing as Zinn," Preston said. "It's the ultimate in hypocrisy and it disgusts the hell out of me."

Breese walked back to the bar and went silent for several minutes. He looked to be pondering something troubling as he settled his tab and drank another round of ice water. Then, all of a sudden, he was in a hurry to go. "How do you know so much about me?" he said.

"I don't," Preston said.

"Stay the hell away from her."

"From who?"

"You know damn well who," Breese said. "Lindy Trego is only friend I've got left and she's selling me out to you."

"Lindy Trego never said a word to me about your breakfasts."

"Who did?"

"None of your business."

Breese snorted at him and was gone, up the hallway to the lobby. A few minutes later, his whale of a car rolled out of the parking lot, heading south.

Preston went into the storage alcove and pulled Breese's check from the magazine on the rack. He grabbed a pack of matches off the bar, went outside, and walked to the end of the dock. Then he burned the check and dropped the ashes into the lake.

20

The pounding on the side door was fierce, ripping Trego out of a murky dream sometime around midnight. She sprang off the sheet, peeked through the fan in the front window and saw Evan's car in her driveway, engine off, a stream of water from the A/C trickling out of the undercarriage and down into the street. Up in the carport, out of her sight, a box of plastic toys crashed onto the concrete, and then she heard Evan cursing under his breath. Across Saturn Lane, two dogs started to yelp. She pulled on sweats and a T shirt and ran downstairs to the TV room.

"In," he hissed when he saw her through the glass. "*Now.*"

His face was contorted with rage. If the girls had been home she would have grabbed her baseball bat and held him at bay. But as his rage dissolved into a pitiful kind of hang-dog pleading, she unbolted the door and backed away quickly as he heaved himself up the steps and inside.

It had been a month since their last communication, his call the morning of the *Citizen* story on Zinn's lunch in Akron. Judging from the way he looked tonight, life had done him no favors since.

"What are you doing here?" she said.

"Like I've been telling you. We need to talk."

"You roused the whole neighborhood," she said. "Can you calm down?"

"Can you offer me a seat?"

After a moment, she pointed toward the kitchen table, and he slumped into the chair in front of the sunflower placemat. "I was just up in Sandusky," he said. "At Preston's fundraiser."

"That's a bit of a shocker," she said. "What's your business with Preston?"

"What's *your's?*"

Trego reached into the refrigerator, pulled out a can of Coke Classic and handed it to him. "I'm avoiding him," she said. "Like I'm avoiding you and her and Zinn and the rest of the crap."

Breese laid his Coke on the placemat without opening it. "Preston doesn't trust me," he said.

"Because you're tied at the hip to her," she said. "You run up to Christopher's every morning and tell her everything you know."

"I'm going to need his vote on Ways & Means in the lame duck. And he doesn't want to give it to me."

"Why would he? You just down-lowed him in his primary."

"Do you *really* believe that?"

"You've never come clean with me—and I can't prove it. But yeah, I believe it."

"Preston knows about our breakfasts."

"Not from me he doesn't," Trego said. "We talk about taxes and working out."

"Pillow talk after a hot fuck?"

"I wish."

Breese stood up, shoved back from the table hard, and knocked over the flower vase, sending water cascading onto the floor. "I paid you to get *him* to run his mouth."

"I quit—remember?"

"And you end up running your own."

"Bullshit, Evan. You're drunk."

Breese pointed his finger at her. "You're hot for him and you blabbed."

"Shit-faced, slobbering drunk."

"After everything I've done for you."

"If I squeal on you, I squeal on myself."

"What *did* you tell him?"

"Nothing," Trego said. "And I didn't sleep with him."

"But you want to."

"So what if I do?"

"Do it then," Breese said. "And when you're done with him you can work through the entire Ways & Means Committee. Spread your cunny out on the witness table in C-5."

She went to the sink to get paper towels to wipe up the water, and as she turned back around Breese fired the can of Coke at her. It hit her square in the forehead. She felt a stabbing pain above her left eye, and then in one deft move he lunged at her and shoved her back into the stove and onto the floor.

He straddled her and pinned her down with his bulk. "I'm trying to help you!" he screamed into her face.

"Let me up!"

"All I've ever done from the day I met you is try to help you!"

"You're breaking my arm!"

He lifted himself up off of her and teetered into the TV room. He ripped a calendar off the wall, kicked over a floor lamp, then went out the side door. A minute later, he gunned his engine and screeched out of the driveway. Trego went in the TV room, dropped face first onto the couch, and sobbed.

Sometime later she heard noises outside and sat up. Through the open door she saw two police officers in the carport. One of them, a young, husky blonde woman, came inside and sat down on the couch next to her.

"Your neighbors heard the commotion and called us," she said. "Are you all right?"

"I think so."

The officer leaned in close to Trego's face and winced. She went to the kitchen, dumped a bunch of ice cubes into a baggie, came back into the TV room and pressed it against Trego's forehead. "What happened?"

Trego didn't reveal much. She'd let an ex-boyfriend inside against her better judgment, he went off on her, she was lucky because her kids weren't home and it could have been worse.

The officer stood up off the couch. "Is he out there driving drunk now?"

"He wasn't drunk."

"Do you want to file a complaint?"

"No."

The officer handed her a business card. "Feel free to contact me if you change your mind. Or if you have questions."

"Thank you."

"Is there anything more I can do for you right now?"

"No."

"Good night, ma'am. And good luck."

*   *   *

On Wednesday, she ate lunch at the Capital Club with the rest of the government relations department at her firm. With the House and Senate in recess, the place was half-empty, but over in a corner she spotted Zinn, of all people, getting rowdy with a group of men she didn't recognize.

When the meal was over her co-workers trooped back to the office, and she stopped upstairs at Fitness Central to retrieve a pair of glasses she'd left in a locker the day before. When she came back down and ran to catch a closing elevator, an arm reached out and shoved the door back open for her. It was one of the men from Zinn's table, a squat, bowling ball of a man in a brown suit. His body reeked of alcohol, tobacco, and un-deodorized sweat.

The door slid shut and they were alone.

"We know each other," he said. "Am I right?"

She told him her first name and the firm she worked for.

"Ah, yes," the man said. "Representative Zinn was just talking about you. You come to Ways & Means."

"Right."

"And sit near the front."

"Usually."

"And take down detailed notes on *everything* he says."

"I didn't know Representative Zinn was so interested in me."

The man giggled like a schoolboy. "He had very nice things to say about your skills outside the office, too. Oral, and so on."

"You're an asshole, mister."

"He's hoping to hook up with you again soon." The man stared greedily at her crotch, then at her bright red face. "You were the one with Preston, up in Akron. You tried to crash our lunch."

"Not me."

"Are you Preston's piece then?" The man belched into the space between them. "It's coming back to me now. You're not Preston's or Zinn's. You're *Breese's*."

"Fuck you."

"What happened to your forehead?"

The elevator opened. He went one way, she the other. Back at work, she closed her door and cried for an hour.

*   *   *

Early Friday morning, Trego's boss popped his head into her office. "Got a minute?" he said.

She followed him down the corridor into the lead partner's corner suite overlooking the Statehouse. The three of them sat down at an enormous table, on which there was absolutely nothing except her trembling hands.

The lead partner gazed at her sadly. "I'm sorry to have to tell you this," he said. "But we're letting you go."

"Why?"

"Several of our clients are quite concerned about you and Evan Breese."

"I have nothing to do with Evan Breese anymore," Trego said.

"We understand that," the lead partner said. He dug his thumb into the underside of this chin. "It's perception that matters. That's what we're up against."

"I'm single," Trego said. "I've got a mortgage to pay and two daughters to support."

"And I've got a law firm to run. We've got clients demanding results. Your presence here is hindering our ability to deliver them."

"You're creating a problem that doesn't exist."

"We've learned a great deal about him—and you—in the last couple of weeks," the lead partner said. "So don't tell me *I'm* creating the problem."

"Do I get a chance to say anything?" Trego said.

"Did you work for Breese for four years?"

"Yes. I told you that in my interview."

"Did he give honorariums to reps who came to his breakfasts?"

"Yes."

"Including Mary Lou Harkins?"

"Her and many more."

"How did you list those payments on Breese's disclosure reports?"

"The way he told me to."

"Which was?"

"Don't list them at all," Trego said. "He told me they didn't have to be there."

The lead partner snorted in disgust. "He's dead-ass wrong," he said. "Lobbyists have to report what they spend and who they spend it on."

"The oversight on lobbyist spending is non-existent," Trego said. "We all know that."

"What good does that do us now?' the lead partner said.

"I've read dozens of reports with my own eyes that reveal nothing," Trego said.

Her boss spoke for the first time. "Some of us do our dead level best to comply with the law," he said. "And apparently some of us don't."

"So why do you have to fire me?"

"The *Citizen* is after Breese," her boss said. "Zinn was their first kill and they want more. They're gunning for Harkins, and you and Breese are going to get dragged in."

"Not if I have anything to say about it."

The lead partner snorted again. "You *don't*. Haven't you figured that out?"

"Would you do this to a man?"

The lead partner stood up and stared at her. "What kind of asinine question is that?"

"Would you be firing me right now if I were a man?"

"Of course I would," the lead partner said. "If he was dumb enough to do what you did. For what—four fucking years?"

She went to the couch at the other end of the office and sat down on it, with her face shielded from the men. Almost immediately, she broke down, and the sobs came violently, leaving her gasping for breath.

The lead partner grabbed a valise off his desk. He touched Trego's boss on the elbow and whispered into his ear. "I have to go," he said. "Keep her in here until she calms down."

"Yes, sir."

"What's with her forehead?"

"Nobody knows."

"Give her four weeks severance and help her box her things up."

"What about health insurance?"

"Terminate coverage. And get her off the premises by nine o'clock."

21

From her seat behind the steering wheel, the Speaker stared at Trego across the interior of the Ford Explorer SUV. It was a look of such fury that Trego wanted to jerk the passenger door open and flee out of the parking garage adjacent to the Union Plaza, and from there to O.J.'s white Bronco or Ted Bundy's Volkswagen or even through the gates of hell itself. Any of those had to be better than here, four feet away from this nightmare of a woman, who looked as angry as Trego had ever in her life seen a human being look.

Her urge to flee was overpowered by a stronger one to stay. Because if, after coming this far, she backed down at the moment of truth, she would have a very hard time forgiving herself.

Two weeks after being fired, she finally had the Speaker face-to-face, cornered really, alone and unprotected. When she'd burst out from behind a parked van and pounded on the SUV's windshield, the vamp's first impulse had no doubt been to step out and ground Trego's face through the glass. Instead, after a long moment of delay, she'd let her inside the grotesquely huge vehicle. The Honorable Mary Lou Harkins must have come to the conclusion that her best option at this point was to sit still, with the engine off and the windows rolled up, and listen to what she had to say.

"Nobody will believe a word of what you're telling me," the Speaker said. "A peon making what—thirty grand a year?"

"I'm the only person they *will* believe."

"A secretary with some bullshit title. A glorified gofer."

"That's what I am," Trego said. "But I'm a gofer who knows about Zinn's money-for-nothing check that he never gave back."

"That had nothing to with me."

"About the breakfasts you came to at Evan's solo firm," Trego said. "Twenty thousand dollars under the radar over four years."

"I earned that money."

"Braun and Lynch and DeRoberts, too. You were all working the gravy train. I've schlepped a lot of high-powered plates in my time."

"Evan botched those reports at his end—*your* end. I didn't do anything wrong."

"Zinn has been screaming from day one that he's a scapegoat," Trego said. "Guess what? He's right."

"What I did was totally legal—and still is."

"This is morality, not legality," Trego said. "I can show the whole world that you and your leadership team are the biggest hypocrites who ever lived. And if I do, it will finish you off in November."

The Speaker flinched. Her face turned chalky white. "I've got a vision someone on your level can't possibly understand," she said.

"I've got a vision too. Evan paying me to funnel money to Deak before the primary."

"I don't know what you're talking about."

"And luring me into your plan to dig up dirt on Jack Preston."

"I don't go after my own," the Speaker said. "Maybe Evan does. Not me."

All around them, drivers arriving for work pulled into spaces and got out of their cars. To avoid being recognized, the Speaker turned her head toward Trego and pulled the big, loose hood of her windbreaker up over her hair.

"Why don't you just get me a job?" Trego said. "As much shit as I can dump on your head, that's *all* I'm asking for. Nine-to-five, away from the Statehouse, out of politics. You can find one for me in an hour."

"Why are you making it so easy for me?"

"Because after all this I still believe in you," Trego said. "In you and the caucus and what you stand for. I'm trying to look past your failures as a human being and focus on the great changes you've brought to the state."

"You've kept your mouth shut so far."

"That was before Evan threw me around in my kitchen," Trego said. "Before Zinn told his lunch buddies how good I am at sucking cock."

"Evan wouldn't hurt a flea. Robby would *never* talk about a woman that way—*any* woman."

"Before I got fired from the best job I'll ever have for no reason."

"You're not blameless in this," the Speaker said.

"Don't you think I know that? I walked by red flags every day with Evan and rationalized them all because he was fighting the good fight."

"He still is."

"Because we were right and the other guys were wrong," Trego said. "Because the end always justifies the means."

"Spare me your soul searching," the Speaker said. "There's nothing more pathetic than a jilted fiancé."

"I dumped Evan. He didn't dump me."

"Go ask him for a job. I don't think I've got one for you."

"I'll just play dumb then," Trego said. "Tell the *Citizen* everything I know with a stupid smile on my face."

"Get out of my car now."

"I'm just a secretary with a bullshit title. I do stupid smiles real well."

She yanked the door open and dropped onto the pavement. "I want to hear from you tomorrow," she said. "Do you understand?"

Almost imperceptibly, the Speaker nodded her head.

"By five o'clock," Trego said. Shivering with fear, she slammed the door.

*   *   *

The next afternoon, while she washed windows on Saturn Lane, her phone rang.

"Bob Dane. Department of Liquor Control."

"Hello."

"We have a position here in our permitting department that we need to fill quickly. We understand you might be interested."

"I am."

"Can you come in for an interview tomorrow?"

She started the following Monday. By the end of the week, she had three voice mail messages from Jana Jacoby, each of them asking if she wanted to sit down and talk about her time with Evan Breese, her new job and why she left her old one, and anything else that might be on her mind.

Trego erased them all.

22

On Tomahawk Trail in Shawnee Hills, the Speaker said good night to the last of fifty friends and family who had spent the Saturday before Labor Day picnicking at the Harkins homestead to kick off her re-election campaign. In the garage, the catering crew bagged trash and stacked tables and chairs, and in the kitchen they loaded leftovers into boxes for delivery to the VFW food pantry. On the lower level, her two sons and their girlfriends settled in for an overnight before they headed back to Washington in the morning, and in the upstairs living room Cubby, blessed Cubby, ramped up college football on the new wide screen unit she'd bought him for his fifty-fifth birthday.

He'd already left the picnic behind and crawled into his cave. She would have to engage him immediately, before he slipped down so deeply into the crevices that they lost all touch. She tossed off her shoes, slid up the stairway, swooped in behind his recliner and planted a kiss on the hairless crown of his head. He twitched, twisted around in his seat, and shot her a wary look.

"What brought that on?" he said.

"Things went well, don't you think?"

"Whatever you say."

"Are you going to be a sourpuss tonight?"

"Are you going to bother me?"

"Three questions," she said. "Then I swear on Granny's Bible, I'll leave you alone."

He fiddled with the remote, and she studied his ruddy face and soulful brown eyes, not much different after four decades from the face and eyes she'd fallen for hard as a high school freshman. The body was well-preserved, too. He hadn't gained five pounds since their wedding day, a blessing for which she was deeply grateful. She shuddered to think how her life might have turned out if Cubby had let himself go to fat.

"The boys are taking two weeks off from work to come home in October," she said. "Isn't that fabulous?"

"Yes, it is."

"You know what would be more fabulous?"

"Tell me."

"If you were here with us."

Eyes fixed on the screen, Cubby jerked his recliner upright, uncapped a bottle of Jim Beam on the end table and poured a shot. "That's a tall order," he said.

"Would you at least think about it?"

"I've got deals bubbling down there. A couple of big office buildings we're trying to close on."

"Could you go back and close this month and drive up here in October? The boys would love it."

"I've had my fill of the boys," Cubby said.

"Could you mute that thing?"

"And they've had their fill of me. It might work better if it's just the three of you."

"No, it wouldn't."

"You see, I pretty much raised them," Cubby said. "Kept them out of the stir from sixth grade all the way up through college."

"You did a magnificent job."

"Off drugs and booze as long as I could," Cubby said. "Which was not *long*—as you *know*—given genetics, family tradition and so forth."

"A better job than I could have," she said. "I don't think I've ever told you that."

"While you've been off making history—first woman *this*, first woman *that*. Cavorting all over the state with your band of brothers."

"*Cavorting*? They aren't exactly a barrel of fun."

"Neither were our beloved offspring," Cubby said. "I had to ride their butts a wee bit hard. Maybe they've told you some stories."

"They have."

"Seems I left some hurt feelings along the way."

"You did."

Cubby drained the shot of Beam. "So I can assure you the boys are about sick to death of my face," he said. "They're not looking for more quality time with the old man."

"Is that what's eating you?"

"That, and every time I get involved in your campaigns you shove me into some hoity-doity restaurant and act rude to me."

"You can be here, eat in front of your TV every night."

"Stick me with your chic, liberal friends and then proceed to call me a hick."

"That was a joke and you know it," she said. "There's only one hick in this house, and it's me. John Culbertson Harkins the Third is no hick."

"Then why did you call me one?"

"It won't happen again" she said. "I promise."

"Uh-oh," Cubby said. "A minute ago you were swearing on Granny's Bible. Now you're just promising."

She bopped his crown with her fist and pushed away from the recliner. "A minute ago we were having a real conversation," she said. "Now you're just talking shit. You must be hammered."

"Am I idiot enough to get hammered in front of your best friends at your kickoff picnic?"

"No."

He poured another shot. "What I'm going to do is get hammered *now*."

"Will you come up in October then?'

He looked away from her and drank the shot down. "I have taken your request under advisement," he said. "I will render my decision tomorrow."

She yanked the remote out of his hands, muted the TV, and dropped onto the foot stand in front of the recliner. "Question two," she said. "Am I in trouble?"

"I couldn't tell you," he said. "I live in Sarasota now."

"Can this goof actually beat me? This insect with rotten teeth and piss stains all over his pants?"

Cubby got out of the recliner, eased around her, and went to adjust some buttons and knobs on the back of the TV. "People are fed up with Ds," he said.

"That's what scares me."

"They're going to vote against Ds just because they're Ds."

"I know they are."

"It's too bad our gallant commander-in-chief in the White House has a zipper problem. He's ticking off a load of folks."

"Torp is flooding the airwaves with the vilest garbage I've ever seen."

"And he's saving a pile of cash to throw at *you*. So yeah—I think Mister Piss Stains *could*—just *possibly*—beat you."

"That's why I need you here."

Cubby came out from behind the TV and stared at her, annoyed. "I made my contacts already," he said. "Got early money for you. As much as I always do."

"You're the only one who did."

He returned to his buttons and knobs. "Can't you get off my back then?"

"Am I that heavy?"

"And these reporters," he said. "Some sexy young thing from the *Citizen* was down there, hanging around the bar at my golf course. Snooping into my personal life."

"I'm sorry."

"Making all kinds of property record requests at the courthouse."

"I don't want you involved in this."

"They're not going to pry a goddam thing out of me," Cubby said. "Don't worry about that."

"Question three," she said. "How can I keep Torp from taking over the House? I've screwed this up so badly I can't see straight anymore."

"You mean cutting Robby too much of a break?"

"Yes."

"Hiring all these private dicks to spy on your own people?"

"Yes."

"Letting the honorarium racket get out of hand?"

"Me and the leadership team bowed out of it years ago," she said. "We should have put the kabosh on it for everybody right then."

Cubby turned the volume up on the TV and stood in front of it, watching the screen. "At this point, I'm not sure you *can* stop Torp," he said. "Seems like your best hope is this CLEAN bill everybody's talking about."

"Jesus, don't say that."

"Call the House back into special session right now and pass it."

"The caucus will go ape shit," she said. "They despise that bill."

"They're a bunch of politicians bitching about losing their perks," Cubby said. "That's all the *more* reason to jump on it."

"I'm not sure I *can* pass it," she said. "Or if the Senate will go along."

"They'll hop on board if you take the lead," Cubby said. "Get with Barbara and what's his name. The young guy."

"I'd rather jam a machete in my stomach than get with those two."

"Hey, girl. If you can't beat um, join um."

She went into her office, pulled Granny's Bible off the top shelf of the bookcase, and went back into Cubby's cave. She stood in front of his screen, opened the Bible, and placed her right hand across the pages.

"I do solemnly swear to leave my husband alone."

She didn't, though. Around one, after the noise on the lower level subsided, she left her office and went over to the bedroom and found him up in the loft, dozing on the cot with his earphones on. She stripped naked, raised up his golden rope with her lips and tongue, and requested a no-frills missionary. He pulled his earphones off and complied, with zest, and it was exquisite to feel his taut torso thrusting on her for once, instead of Evan's suffocating bulk.

A few hours before sunrise, after they'd climbed down from the loft into bed, he woke her up and they went another round.

*   *   *

She got up early and cooked breakfast for everyone, and after they saw the boys and their friends off, she and Cubby went into town for the eleven o'clock service at Trinity United Methodist. When they got home, his van was in the parking space next to the kitchen, and the yard boys were loading his wide-screen unit into the back.

"I hope you don't mind," he said. "I need one down there."

"Taking off soon?"

"In an hour or two. And I won't be coming back in October."

She felt a flush of anger at his unrelenting bitterness. "I've treated you like a piece of crap all these years," she said. "So you're going to even the score by deserting me in my hour of need."

"Don't get all melodramatic," he said. "It's just that you're better off without me."

"You know that's not true."

"I'll cause a ruckus," he said. "Punch some reporter through a window."

"You've never done that before."

"That just means I'm due," he said. "You've got an image problem and I'm a big part of it. So it's best I make myself scarce. Besides, I *finally* got a bit of a life down there."

"I can see that."

"I actually *want* to go back."

"Sounds like a girlfriend."

"Fair is fair."

"Anybody I know?"

"Remember our rule. Don't ask, don't tell."

He left an hour later. The Speaker spent the rest of the afternoon in her garden, patching soil and harvesting cucumbers and carrots.

23

Eleanor "Mac" McKenzie, the 33rd richest woman in America and publisher of the *Citizen*, emerged from the restroom on the second level of the Hyatt on Capitol Square and walked toward the ballroom, where cocktail hour at the black-tie fundraiser for Friends of Metro Library was in full swing. She paused to say hello to a friend, and as she turned back around she saw Jacoby, bearing down on her like some kind of she-wolf. She'd no doubt snuck up the back escalator, away from the crowd, and found McKenzie here exactly as she wanted her—weary and wistful, more intoxicated than she'd planned to be, and not at all eager to join her husband and their table for two hours of chatter, cold food, and soporific speeches from a host of civic leaders.

Inclined, that is, to indulge a stunning girl with a pressing agenda item, especially one with the instincts and chutzpah to track her down on the evening shift. The executive editor had called her at three o'clock to relay the message from the bureau chief that Jacoby was indignant, and capable of doing something rash.

Apparently, this was it.

"Ms. McKenzie."

"Ms. Jacoby. What a surprise."

"Before you go in, may I speak with you?"

"Let's make it brief, shall we?"

"I'm disappointed in your decision to kill our piece."

"An easy call, I assure you."

"Will you reconsider?"

"The editors and your bureau chief and I met this afternoon," McKenzie said. "We've agreed to shelve it and move on."

Jacoby wrapped a hand around her wrist, and she felt her loins surge. The belly and bush of a favorite lover from fifty years ago appeared in her mind's eye, and what little resistance she might have been able to muster melted away. Then Jacoby was leading her to the back end of the floor, away from onlookers, and into a dark, empty meeting room, where they sat down on plastic chairs.

"We've worked on this story for months," Jacoby said. "Reviewed hundreds of documents. Interviewed thirty sources."

"And come up with nothing of real substance."

"I beg to differ."

"Running what you've got on Mary Lou Harkins is not my idea of responsible journalism," McKenzie said.

"We didn't pay anybody for information," Jacoby said.

"It belongs in the *National Enquirer*, not the *Citizen*."

"Stake them out like cops or rifle through their trash."

"And you won't," McKenzie said. "Not as long as I'm running the ship."

"Mary Lou Harkins abuses her power," Jacoby said.

"Don't they all?"

"She rages like an animal at her staff."

"Of that I have no doubt."

"She blackmails her friends, extorts money from everybody who walks into her office."

McKenzie let out a rueful laugh. "You *could* say the same thing about me."

"She also uses cocaine."

"Are you using with her?"

"Of course not."

"Then how do you know?"

"We have three eyewitness accounts."

"All anonymous," McKenzie said.

"Including the Mt. Adams Fish House in Cincinnati in June. She was snorting lines in the upstairs bathroom during a fundraising dinner."

"We don't do anonymous."

"Mary Lou Harkins is an evil human being," Jacoby said. "She's presiding over an utterly corrupt pay-to-play system and she threw Zinn under the bus to hide her own involvement. We've got a moral obligation to inform the public. If we don't, who will?"

She had to give the young woman her due. She was as relentless and self-assured as any reporter the *Citizen* had ever employed. McKenzie had a wayward granddaughter the same age as Jacoby who could barely bathe and clothe herself. The gap between their maturity levels astonished her; it was as wide as the Grand Canyon.

Jacoby gave her a piercing look. "Are you killing this piece because Mary Lou Harkins is a woman? Because she's pro-choice and you are, too?"

McKenzie's blood pressure spiked a couple of notches. "I'm killing this piece because we don't have enough facts to run it."

"Are you scared of her?" Jacoby said. "I'd hate to think the owner of Ohio's greatest newspaper is backing down because she might get hurt."

"You have a naïve view of the world."

"How so?"

"My husband loves me," McKenzie said. "And I love him. I'm as healthy as a horse, and I've got 242 million dollars in the bank. What can some politician *possibly* do to hurt me?"

Jacoby blushed and looked at the floor, and she was gratified to see she'd chastened her, knocked her down a rung, if only for the moment.

"Your chief tells me Zinn is going to be indicted in Cincinnati."

"The law firms wouldn't talk to the Ethics Committee," Jacoby said. "But they went to the prosecutor. He's being charged with two counts of receiving unlawful compensation."

"And you've nailed Breese to the wall on his expenditure reports. Made him the poster child of a dysfunctional system."

"In spades," Jacoby said. "With no help at all from his old secretary. It's like she's dropped off the face of the Earth."

"Isn't all of that enough for you?"

"Enough?"

"To satisfy your blood lust."

Jacoby frowned and shook her head back and forth hard. "That is *really* unfair."

"I don't follow all the intrigue across the street with *quite* the intensity you do," McKenzie said. "But from my angle it looks like we gave the politicos a pretty hard smack."

"It could have been a harder smack."

McKenzie stood up. "Maybe our stories will help get CLEAN passed," she said.

"I certainly hope so."

"I must say the spectacle of these people coming into town for a special session is amusing," McKenzie said. "All this huffing and puffing over who can be cleaner than the other."

Jacoby didn't display the barest hint of a smile. She stood up and shook out her thick auburn hair. "I'll be on my way now," she said.

"I deeply respect your skills," McKenzie said.

"Thank you."

"I'm in awe of your tenacity."

"But please," Jacoby said. "Tenacity is not blood lust. I'm not trying to kill anyone. I'm just trying to be the best reporter I can be."

"I hope to have you with us at the *Citizen* for many, many years."

"Enjoy your evening ma'am."

Jacoby left the room, and a few seconds later McKenzie saw her hopping on the back escalator to the lobby. She was running late now; cocktail hour was over and dinner was underway. She walked quickly to the restroom, went into the last stall and closed the door, and brought herself to climax with fifty artful strokes. Then she washed up and headed into the ballroom, wondering if life might have passed her by.

24

In the cafeteria in the basement of the Center, Crissinger, dean of the D caucus, pleaded with Preston as their breakfast orders sizzled on the grill.

"Jack—I need your assistance."

"Anything I can do."

"Come back to my booth and explain to us less enlightened exactly what the hell is going on around here."

"I would if I could."

"Twenty-four years in this place and I've never seen a piece of legislation rammed down our throats like this."

The rank-and-file were agitated. Several were rumored to be flirting with open rebellion. Called by the Speaker into special session for the sole purpose of passing CLEAN, dragged away from home in the midst of their general election campaigns, they had spent three days twiddling their thumbs as they waited for Hyams and the Ethics Committee to craft the version of the bill that would be sent to the floor for a vote.

The Speaker was talking with each D individually to soothe fears, shore up support, and seek additional co-sponsors. From Preston's perspective, all of that cajoling would be needed to get CLEAN through the House.

"It's the only medicine for what ails us," Preston said.

"Then why do I feel like horse shit from hell?"

"Count your blessings," Preston said. "You could be Zinn."

"He's getting what he deserves," Crissinger said. "Maybe the judge down there will lock him up, get him out of our hair."

"Or Breese."

"I never grasped the allure of that man," Crissinger said. "Three years ago he was walking on water. What's he done lately?"

"All he's doing at the moment is hiding."

"What I'm pulling out of the *Citizen* is, he's looking at a dozen misdemeanor counts," he said. "Is that it?"

"Correct," Preston said. "For failure to file accurate and timely expenditure reports."

Crissinger smiled wanly. "I've taken more than a few checks from Breese over the years," he said in a low voice. "All I can say is, there for the grace of God go I."

Back in the booth, Ash and Kaminski scanned the morning papers and chowed down on scrambled eggs and sausage. They eyed Preston glumly as he sat down.

"I've invited Jack to give us the inside scoop," Crissinger said. "I *know* he's got it."

Ash crossed his thick forearms, leaned back from his plate, and eyeballed Preston. "Well, Mr. CLEAN, are you happy?"

"As a lark," Preston said. "Can't you tell?"

"You're going to get what you want," Ash said. "A House full of goo-goos. Idealists clinging to the quaint notion that you can keep money out of politics."

"It's time to change the way we do business," Preston said.

Ash shook his head. "Even if we could keep it out—why *should* we?"

"Are you for sale—or rent?"

"Money runs every other aspect of society," Ash said. "How can you expect it *not* to run politics?"

Kaminski cut his sausage into chunklets with a white plastic knife. "Nobody had a problem until Zinn got greedy and ruined things for everyone," he said. "It was a nice set-up, Jack. You can understand why people are upset."

"Can you embrace the idea that passing CLEAN might *help* us?" Preston said.

Ash burst into a thunderous laugh that turned heads in the room. "Some of us have to *work* to get re-elected," he said loudly. "And we can't get much done sitting here in Columbus, waiting to pass this bill voters don't give a damn about."

Kaminski let out a long, sad sigh. "United Way is holding their breakfast bash at the YWCA today," he said. "I've gone for ten years. If it wasn't for all the heat from media over this thing, that's where I'd be now."

"Ditto," Ash said.

"Listening," Kaminski said. "Learning, picking up good information."

"Doing our *jobs,*" Ash said. "Imagine that."

Kaminski wiped his hands with a napkin, balled it up and tossed it on his plate. After moaning a bit longer about the dismal state of affairs they were in, he and Ash scooted out of the booth and headed upstairs.

"Sorry, Jack," Crissinger said. "I didn't mean to lead you into an ambush."

"No sweat," Preston said. "I've got my flak jacket on."

"Better keep it on."

*   *   *

At two o'clock, he was summoned to the Speaker's office for what he presumed would be a one-on-one meeting, and was surprised to find Braun, DeRoberts and Lynch with her. He had not conversed with the Speaker for five months, since the morning in April when she'd reamed him out in her suite at the Union Plaza over the Jacoby interview.

Perhaps she'd called in the leadership team because she couldn't stomach the thought of being alone in the same room with him. That was understandable; he felt the same way about her. He'd been dreading their encounter and welcomed the presence of the others. He sat down with the three of them around the coffee table.

"Speaker Harkins is replacing you as lead co-sponsor of CLEAN," Braun said. "Chair Hyams will stay on as chief sponsor. The Speaker's name will be listed at the top of the title next to hers."

"Where does that put me?" Preston said. "Out in the gutter?"

"Down the page, with the rest of the caucus," Lynch said. "We've got forty now and we think we'll have everybody on board by the time we get to the floor."

"Try to understand, this isn't personal," Braun said.

"It's hard to think otherwise," Preston said.

From behind her big desk, the Speaker stared dully at him. She looked emaciated, as if she'd consumed nothing but lettuce and saltines for a month. Maybe stress was the cause, or some type of medication that was suppressing her appetite. Or perhaps the whisperings that he had heard from Waiters and Entrekin and his secretary were true, and she was binging on cocaine. That scenario, which he didn't believe to be true, was too disturbing to dwell on.

"Why did you change your mind on this?" Preston said to her.

"Because I realized you were right," the Speaker said.

"Did you figure out that this is the only way to wipe the muck of Zinn off us?"

"Zinn is not relevant to this discussion," DeRoberts said. "We're leaving him to the court in Cincinnati—and the voters."

"Let them finish the job we didn't have the guts to," Preston said.

"We're talking about the *bill*," DeRoberts said. "Ethics will report it Thursday. We'll pass it Friday and ship it to the Senate. They'll move next week, we'll hash out our differences, and the Governor will sign it."

"It's an emergency measure and will be effective immediately upon his signature," Lynch said. "We'll have the strictest ethics law in the country in two weeks."

"No more honorariums," DeRoberts said. "Full disclosure of *all* lobbyist expenditures on public officials. Real oversight for the first time."

"Where is Torp?" Preston said.

"With us," Braun said. "Every other R will be with him."

"I'll believe that when I see it," Preston said.

"They threw down the gauntlet and we ran through it," Braun said. "They've got no choice but to follow."

"They won't be bobbing and feinting like they did on the Zinn vote," DeRoberts said. He looked at Preston. "And we trust *you* won't be either."

"CLEAN has my full and unequivocal support," Preston said.

"One more thing before you go," Lynch said.

He handed Preston a one-page memo. It contained a list of twelve individuals, union locals, companies and non-profit agencies in the 53rd District, including several that had contributed to Preston's campaign.

"We need your help with fundraising," Lynch said.

"I'm not sure how much I can give you."

"You've got an easy race," DeRoberts said. "You're going to win by fifteen points or more."

"I am?"

"We think you can deliver at least twenty thousand to the leadership fund from these sources," DeRoberts said.

"I can barely deliver that to myself."

"Have you *tried*?" DeRoberts said. "You might be better at it than you think."

"I hate asking people for money," Preston said.

Braun hissed at him. "So does everybody else."

"I hate it so much I'm not even asking you all for help," Preston said. "I'm not costing you one red cent. Why can't that be my contribution?"

"This is an unprecedented situation," DeRoberts said. "We're in the fight of our lives and we need you to get involved as soon as possible."

"Breese is dying on the vine," Lynch said. "He's losing clients every day and delivering nothing to us. And Zinn is in free fall."

"The trial lawyers and Teamsters are scaling back," DeRoberts said. "Even the *teachers* are shorting us."

Preston could not suppress a snicker. "Things are so dire you're enlisting *me* to save the day?"

"We're asking our underachievers to step up to the plate," Braun said. "You're one of them."

"We've got nine or ten guys who aren't getting what they need to be getting," Lynch said. "We need to lift them up."

"I understand now," Preston said. "We share the wealth— like Huey Long. Every man is a king—and no one wears a crown."

"Smart ass," DeRoberts said. He buzzed Preston with angry eyes.

"So we pass CLEAN—with the Speaker's name at the top of the page to make sure everybody sees it," Preston said. "Then we take a quick bow to the press and get on with the business of saving the majority."

From behind her desk, the Speaker spoke up in a loud voice. "You can pitch in," she said. "Or you can stand on the sidelines and sneer at everybody who does."

"I want to mull this for a while," Preston said.

"We can't afford that," DeRoberts said.

"Jack—it's nut cutting time," the Speaker said. She looked quite angry now. "Are you going to be part of the problem—or part of the solution?"

Blindsided and outnumbered, Preston stood up, tucked the memo into his shirt pocket and left the office without saying another word. Outside, he found Crissinger in front of the big map, wringing his hands, waiting to be called in.

"Is she cracking the whip?"

"Take off your shirt and kneel down," Preston said. "Prepare yourself for twenty lashes."

"I'm an old guy," Crissinger said. "My time is short. Maybe she'll go easy on me."

25

On October 5th, a month and three days before the general election, the Governor was scheduled to sign CLEAN at eleven o'clock in the Statehouse Atrium. Twenty minutes before the start of the ceremony, in a small library on the lower level, Hyams took a moment alone to gather her thoughts before heading upstairs to join legislative leaders, media, and forty invited guests assembling in the main hall to usher in what was being hailed as a new era on Capitol Square.

Hyams knew that the claims being made for the bill's momentousness were exaggerated. The ordeal of the last four weeks had forced her to admit that Evan Breese was right. There was no way to eliminate unethical behavior. The best way to stop abuse was to put into law that the abuse must stop. But that would not be enough. No matter how many loopholes were closed—and CLEAN closed virtually all of them—people would discover ways to circumvent the rules. At that moment, lawyers ensconced in the towers of commerce surrounding them were doing exactly that.

Despite those misgivings, the ceremony would be a moment of triumph. In her last year in office, at the end of a largely undistinguished career, she had moved past the Speaker's odious behavior toward her during the Zinn hearings, seized the moment, and forged a legacy. Managing the bill in the House, then negotiating in conference committee with the Senate to reach consensus on a number of contentious issues, she had come away with a piece of legislation that would do more to alter the mores of the state's political class than any law ever passed.

A rustle at the open door interrupted her reflections. It was Preston, more dapper that she'd ever seen him, decked out in a finely cut charcoal gray suit, a blue silk tie and a pair of glistening black wingtips. He'd even shortened up his scruffy hair into something approaching a Marine brush cut. The wire rim glasses were still there, along with the hard, slender body and quizzical look he liked to affect. But all the rest of him seemed bright and new.

"Is that the gentleman from the 53rd District?"

"Reporting for duty."

"I hardly recognized you."

"I'm cleaning up my act," Preston said. "Joining the establishment."

It looked good on him. He came into the room and sat down at the far end of the big oak table, in front of the bookcase that held the maroon volumes of the Revised Code. Her appraisal of him had not changed in the six months since their encounter at the Hayes Center in Fremont before the primary. He was a comer, smart and passionate about policy *and* politics, capable of excelling at the inside game within the Statehouse and the outside one everywhere else. Bringing him into the inner circle of decision-makers on CLEAN would have been overreaching. Volatile, prone to pettiness, fixated on his utopian ideal of how government should be run, he wasn't ready for high-level work on a major bill. That was one thing she and leadership had agreed on.

But those shortcomings could be addressed—and surmounted. With CLEAN enacted, and the future of the caucus precarious, Preston was definitely an asset to be nurtured.

"Thank you for getting me into the ceremony," he said.

"I convinced her it was the right thing to do."

"That took some effort, I'm sure."

"Not really," Hyams said. "I think she's ready to forgive you and bring you back into the fold."

"It must be the money I'm raising for the caucus."

"You—raising money?"

"I got over my hang-ups about purity and made the contacts leadership asked me to," Preston said. "Put suspicion and resentment and anger aside and did what's best for the group."

"I bet you made out better than you thought you would."

Preston blushed. "I'm delivering five checks for five thousand apiece to Lynch after the ceremony."

"And now that you're giving, do you want to give more?"

"I never imagined myself saying this—but yes. And it's confusing the heck out of me because I'm not supposed to feel that way."

"How are you supposed to feel?"

"Like I betrayed myself."

"You did nothing of the kind," Hyams said. "Attending to the political side of your job is necessary."

"Tell me something," Preston said. "Why did everybody bitch to high heaven behind closed doors about this bill and then vote yes?"

"Hard-bitten practicality," Hyams said. "Either vote yes or head into October with a ten-ton albatross around your neck."

"Will passing it save the majority for us?"

"If they couldn't knock us out two years ago, why now?" Hyams said. "Believe me, you wouldn't like being in the minority,"

"Either way, we're going to have to live with these new rules."

"It would be a horrible thing to face," Hyams said. "Some of our guys would quit before their terms were out. They wouldn't be able to deal with being cut off at the knees."

"What are you doing next year?" Preston said.

"I'm going to run the Center for Ethics and Excellence at Case Western in Cleveland."

"Can I share that information?"

"Please don't," Hyams said. "It would just be a distraction."

"I'll miss you."

"I don't have the stomach for it anymore."

"Is she one of the things driving you away?"

"Yes, she is."

"I've seen her anger—up close. I know what she can inflict on people."

"So do I."

"You were upset the day of her fundraiser back in June," Preston said.

"Let's not get into that."

"Crying in the alley behind the Union Plaza," Preston said. "That's what I heard."

A page popped his pimply face in the door. "We're ready to get started," he said.

Hyams stood up and reached her arms across the table.

"Representative Preston, will you escort me upstairs? It's time to join our brothers and sisters."

26

Just off I-70 near the Zanesville Airport, in a room at a Holiday Inn, Breese slapped shaving cream on his neck and cheeks at the sink and listened as the Speaker, spread eagle nude across the king bed, recounted the latest episode of treachery in the caucus.

"Imagine Ash over in Dayton, blabbing about my temper."

"He's not doing any such thing."

"Don't *doubt* me, counselor. I've got connections in Dayton and they don't lie."

"We all lie," Breese said. "Some of us are better at it than others."

"It's six o'clock in the morning. Don't start in on that crap."

"I dropped ten large for Ash last week."

"And he thanks us by telling a bunch of old ladies at some senior center how I dumped a bowl of chili on his head. During tort reform."

"He deserved it."

"And it worked," she said. "Did he switch his vote an hour later or didn't he?"

It was an absurd way to do business—trysting every four or five days on the road, in out-of-the-way locales where few people, if any, might recognize them. He would arrive first and secure the room and refreshments. She'd follow a few hours later in her Explorer, usually at dusk, and slip in like a ghost to join him. Less than three weeks from Election Day, and they were gunning all over creation like a couple of juiced-up kids. But since his paperwork mess had exploded in the *Citizen* and drawn the attention of the prosecutor, that is how she wanted things done.

He wasn't going to raise an objection. Just like always, he would obey his orders. Put on his uniform and march.

She sat up and snorted a line of cocaine off the cover of a phone book. "Preston has been a nice surprise," she said. "I wasn't sure he had the gonads to be a player."

"Now that's he's raised his share, he's being standoffish," Breese said. "He simply refuses to work with me."

"When are you going to raise *your* share?" she said. "That's what I want to know." She snorted another line.

"You ingest way too much of that substance."

"Use it or lose it," she said. She ran her index finger across the phone book to pick up residue, then licked it clean. "I'm not going to carry any out of here."

"Maybe I should cut you off."

"Then I'll cut *yours* off—both of them."

"Make an executive decision for the good of the order."

"Before you do, there's something you should know," she said. "I got the prosecutor to backburner your case."

"That was you?"

"Until January," she said. "She won't even *look* at the file for three months."

"By then my hotshot lawyer will have it all cleared up," Breese said.

"He goddam well better."

"I'll apologize for my bad habits, plead guilty to a couple of misdemeanors, and pay my fines. And that will be the end of that puppy."

"In your dreams, counselor. It won't be anything close to the end. Not if precious Lindy runs her mouth."

"She won't," Breese said. "You gave her what she asked for."

"Too many people remember too much," she said. "And there's always Deak. He could blab any time if somebody leans on him."

Breese picked a wet washcloth off the counter and tossed it playfully at her. "Girlfriend, change your focus," he said. "We've got an election to win."

She extracted the remote from a pile of tangled sheets and began to channel surf. "The boys are coming in this week," she said. "They're going to go door-to-door together for me."

"That'll give you a nice bump."

"What makes you think I need a bump?"

"Is there *anything* I can do to help you down home?"

"Stay away from my district," she said. "Act like you've never met me."

"Do I stink that bad?"

"I'm afraid you do."

"Then I'll take a few days in the office," Breese said. "To catch up."

"Be on your guard," she said. "I have it on good authority that those SOBs are ready to have it out with you."

Breese finished shaving and slung his towel over the shower rack. He climbed into a pair of boxer-briefs, went to the front of the room, and peeked out the curtain next to the door. The first light of dawn was creeping in. Traffic was picking up quickly. He needed to get moving.

"Bring those smooth cheeks over here," she said. She wiped her crotch with the washcloth Breese had thrown at her, then sat up on the edge of the bed. "Because I *hate* it when you scratch my thighs."

Room service has arrived, Breese thought. She leaned back onto her elbows and spread her legs. He dropped to his knees on the floor in front of her and licked gamely. In a minute she was bucking herself gently against his mouth, sucking in air through clenched teeth, exhaling with a hiss. When he sensed she was close he jabbed his tongue into her as deeply as he could. She came with a long, low moan, then half a dozen pelvic thrusts that jarred his head up and off the sweaty blanket.

Forty minutes later, she was at the door, car keys in hand. "Marion, Thursday night," she said. "I'm doing a grip and grin with Florence."

"There's a Travelodge on Mount Gilead Road," he said.

"Look for me around six," she said. "Don't forget my treats."

*   *   *

In a reading nook, on the attic floor of the mansion off Capitol Square that housed Titan Group, Breese listened to his partners Junig and Corrigan trudge up the creaky stairs to confront him. They'd been circling like barracudas all day, and now that everyone was gone for the evening, they'd jumped, just like she'd told him they would. As usual, Junig would play nasty, Corrigan nice.

"This situation is spiraling out of control," Junig said.

"We agreed to ride it out until January," Breese said.

"That was before you lost the Limited account."

"Somebody found out what they were paying me and undercut us," Breese said.

"Bank One and the race track owners, too. How many more are you going to lose?"

"None," Breese said. "And the ones who dumped me will regret it because they're going to need me in the lame duck."

"Are you even going to be in *town* for the lame duck?" Junig said.

"Instead of in jail?" Breese said. "Is that what you mean?"

"You're damaging Titan," Junig said. "I can't get anything done because all anybody wants to talk about is you and when you're going to be indicted."

"My problems have nothing to do with Titan," Breese said.

"Of course they don't," Corrigan said. "We know that."

"My reports have been fine here."

"I wish it were that simple," Junig said. "Unfortunately, it's not."

Breese stood up and put his hands on his hips. "If you want to throw me out, just say so."

"If you had an ounce of honor, you'd resign," Junig said.

Breese stared deep into Junig's hostile eyes. "Don't lecture me about honor," he said. "When the time came for you to serve your country, where were you?"

Corrigan fretted like a nervous mother. "Calm down, Evan."

"*Where?*"

"He doesn't mean what he's saying," Corrigan said.

"Hiding your yellow ass in law school with a student deferment," Breese said.

"Me and a million other guys."

"You sent the son of a working man off to the jungle to die in your place."

"I had other priorities."

"Sure you did," Breese said. "Busting unions, beating up homosexuals. Threatening black people at the polls."

Corrigan looked beside himself. "You're a key part of this firm," he said. "As far as I'm concerned, you're here as long as you want to be."

"I'll be here as long as she's Speaker," Breese said. "Not one second longer."

"This is a struggle for you," Junig said. "We understand that. But don't let your emotions get the better of you."

"January," Breese said. "That's the agreement. Honor it."

"We'll talk again after the election," Junig said.

"I've got a load of work to get done," Breese said. "Why don't you get the hell out of here and let me do it?"

They did.

27

On the night before the election, in her office on Tomahawk Trail, the Speaker prepared to work the phones after an exhausting day of campaigning. In sweat pants, wool socks and a baggy brown pullover, she puffed hard on a Camel Light and stared at the list of calls to be made that she'd taped to the wall under her picture of Vern.

There were many people to thank, more to encourage, and a painfully large number to berate. Most members of the caucus had tried hard to help themselves and their colleagues win re-election. She would inform those who had not that their weak efforts were not appreciated.

Focusing on others gave her less time to dwell on herself. With Evan in Columbus and Cubby in Sarasota, the boys back in D.C. and staff off-duty, she was alone in the house. Alone with sweaty sheets, her call list, and the three grams she'd carried home under the rear seat of her Explorer after a sleepover with Evan at a Days Inn in Coshocton.

She was an atheist. She had left Father, Son and Holy Ghost in the dust bin decades ago and never looked back. But if there was ever a moment in her life that she felt compelled to pray to a higher power, this was it. And she would ask not for victory, but simply for extra strength—the strength she was going to need, win or lose, to make it through the next twenty-four hours.

She snuffed her cigarette into an ashtray and drank a shot of bourbon for courage. As she sat down at her desk, the phone rang. The caller ID flashed *Robert Zinn.* She recoiled in shock and dismay, then snatched up the receiver an instant before the call went into voice mail.

"Robby, is that you?"

She heard labored breathing, then the babbling of infant children and a woman's shushing.

"I've been trying to get through this without inflicting myself on you," Zinn said. "But I'm a weakling."

"No, you're not," she said. "You're the strongest of the strong."

"I want to chair Ways & Means in the lame duck," Zinn said. "Can I have my committee back?"

"I'm surprised to hear you say that."

"It's the moment of truth for tax reform."

"Something is going to come out of Ways & Means," she said. "I don't think it will be that bill."

"Then I'll lift my stuff out of 66 and put it wherever it needs to go."

"You can't do it alone," she said. "Haven't you learned that by now?"

He went away from the phone for a moment, to shoo someone out of the room. When he came back he was eating something. "Win or lose tomorrow, give me my chair back," he said. "Let me do it *right*."

The audacity of his request astonished her. Her plans for the lame duck did not include him in any way, shape, or form, and he knew that. He was a supreme embarrassment now. The best thing he could do at this point was sit in a corner with his mouth shut and do as he was told. He was living in a dream world, as if the last six months—the Damon's lunch, the *Citizen* stories, his reprimand in the House and indictment in Hamilton County—had never occurred.

"I'll stick with Kimball," she said.

"Kimball cannot get it done," he said.

"Neither can you."

"The guns will eat him alive," he said. "You owe it to the people to bring me back."

"Ah, *the people*," she said. "I can hear the mob in my drive-way right now. Screaming give Robby Zinn his committee back."

"And to *me*."

There was dead air between them. She got out of the chair, grabbed the pack of Camel Lights off the top of the file cabinet, and lit another. "You're going to trial in January," she said.

"I'll be acquitted."

"Why would you put yourself through that?"

"Because I'm innocent."

"No, you're not."

"I swear to God I didn't know what checks I was cashing."

"You blew off dinners and went to see the Reds," she said.

"How do you know?"

"Because you sat in the Ferris-Cornell luxury box with twenty other people," she said. "They remember the evenings well because you made such an ass out of yourself."

"You believe this gang of corporate thugs instead of me," he said. "This wacko prosecutor using my case to get his face on TV."

"You did the same thing with Evan."

"There's always Evan to contend with, isn't there?"

"And who knows how many more."

"You and your blubberball boyfriend selling me out," Zinn said. "That makes such perfect sense."

"You sold *all* of us out."

"The two of you, doing some dumb little hillbilly jig over my carcass. Leaving me to rot in the middle of the road."

"Why didn't you let your lawyer work out of a deal?"

"I thought you wanted me to fight," he said. "Mom would have."

"There's a time to fight and a time to lay your weapon down."

"When did you ever fight for me?"

"I kept the caucus from expelling you this summer," she said. "There are plenty who still want to."

"Thieves, liars, self-serving scumbags."

"No, Robby. Remarkable human beings."

"Maybe if you hadn't sold out so *completely,*" Zinn said. "Wrapped your skinny legs around anybody who can raise a buck."

"You're disgusting."

"Yes I am," he said. "But at least I'm not fucking around on my wife."

"You're going to lose tomorrow," she said.

"So are you."

"It isn't even going to be close," she said. "You're finished in politics forever—and you deserve to be."

There was a commotion behind him, then the crash of something heavy hitting the floor. He left the phone again, and this time when he came back he had one of his babies with him, cooing and gurgling into the receiver.

"I may go down tomorrow," he said. "The judge in Cincinnati may throw me in jail. But I'll figure out a way to come out on top in the end."

"You always do."

"I've got my eyes on the prize."

"Go for it."

"I'm going to make Mom very, *very* proud."

He hung up.

*   *   *

The next day, she voted early at the firehouse, then spent the rest of the morning at D headquarters at the Copper Kettle Restaurant on Paint Street, across from the courthouse. She was gratified and reassured by the steady stream of well-wishers, but by noon her nerves were frayed and she drove to Tomahawk Trail alone to call Evan and Lynch and her candidates in the most pivotal races. All she wanted was uplifting data from the exit polls, something tangible to grip in her hand to convince herself that they were going to prevail.

What she got instead stunned her.

If the numbers were any indication of what would transpire later on—and there was no reason to think otherwise—it was going to be the most miserable night of her life.

The polls closed statewide at seven-thirty. By then she had made twenty calls and received twenty more, and the prognosis had gone from miserable to horrific. As expected, Zinn was well on his way to oblivion. But Ash was going down too, the late money from Evan working almost like a curse. Crissinger was neck-and-neck in his own parish, where he needed to be far ahead. In Youngstown, Helvey lost to a disc jockey, and in Toledo, Kaminski was running behind a pro-life, pro-gun Buick dealer in a cowboy hat.

She grew colder and angrier with each fresh piece of bad news. Elmore, Clark and Collier—solid incumbents who'd been expected to win handily—all lost squeakers. Gerrard, who'd gotten complacent in the last month, was defeated by a mediocre has-been who Torp had lured out of retirement. Even Seidenberg, the woman she'd groomed to take over for Hyams, was shocked by an upstart R, whose sole qualification for office seemed to be that he had served a tour of duty in the Gulf War. The most devastating loss of all was Waiters, gone after one term, a loser by six hundred votes to the black, female CEO of a cosmetics company.

At eight-thirty, she abandoned the phones and drove back to the Copper Kettle. Until that moment, she had avoided any news whatsoever on her own race, and when she entered the room she went immediately to the big blackboard up front and read the returns from a dozen key precincts.

In an instant, she knew she was beaten. And the unforgiving truth was that she had been rejected not by voters in the outlying parts of the district, but by her own classmates, neighbors, and friends.

Perhaps they believed they were doing her a favor by sparing her another term, this one served in the powerless minority under thick clouds of suspicion and accusation. Yes, that was the way to think of it. The electors, in their infinite compassion and wisdom, had granted her a reprieve.

Down by six points with ninety-nine percent of the returns verified, she summoned the fortitude to call Mister Piss Stains at ten o'clock and extend her congratulations. When that ordeal was over, she walked slowly to the front of the room and stood erect, impassive, perfectly still. As the two dozen or so die-hard supporters who hadn't left gathered around her, she gave a one-minute concession speech, said thank you and goodnight, and drove home.

She turned off the phones, took a hot shower, and climbed up into the loft above her bedroom. With her treats at her side, she lost herself in the dark woods outside until the sun came up.

28

Forty-eight hours after the close of the polls, Preston leaned on his refrigerator door on Vineyard Circle and hashed over the D debacle with Jana Jacoby. She'd called to congratulate him on his twenty-point re-election victory and to garner, off-the-record as always, his input on the question lurking in everyone's mind: *why?*

"What did you guys do wrong?" she said.

"We didn't do anything wrong."

"Why did the Rs pick up fifteen seats?"

"The voters turned against Democrats."

"It's as simple as that?"

"The people have spoken," Preston said. "We've got no choice but to accept it."

"So eloquent with the party line."

"Our day will come round again," Preston said. "We need to be ready for it when it happens."

"Are you running for minority leader?"

"There isn't much left to lead."

"Your survivors need to hitch their wagon to someone."

"To be a leader at the Statehouse these days you need a mountain of gold," Preston said. "And a very sick mind."

Jacoby laughed. "Friday is my last day at the *Citizen*," she said. "I've got a job with CNN in Washington."

He felt a searing pang of regret. He should have thrown caution and reserve to the wind and tried harder to get to know Jacoby. Maybe she was out of his league, and he was fooling himself. But she was surely beyond his reach now, riding a rocket to the moon, and whatever slim chance he might have had of gaining a piece of her affection was gone forever.

"My God," he said. "The *Athens News* to CNN in what— eight months?"

"More like seven."

"You're not even going to hang around for the lame duck?"

"Nope. I'm leaving town Saturday."

"Why the rush?"

She hesitated. Preston had a glorious vision of her in blue jeans and a dark gray T shirt, curled up on a couch, painting her toenails cherry red.

"There's more to the story of Breese and the Speaker," she said.

"What have you found?"

"Everything under the sun and then some," she said. "I wanted to print it but none of my bosses did."

"We know who won that argument."

"So I'm moving on," she said. "But I'd like to offer you a parting gift. Some confidential information I know you'll be interested in."

"Don't feel obligated."

"I held off until after the election because I didn't want to create a distraction for you."

"Why are you blessing me now?"

"Come *on*, Jack. If it wasn't for you, I'd be back in Athens, covering zoning board meetings. And you showed me the way on Zinn."

"You would have found your own way without me."

She dropped into a low voice, barely above a whisper. "It's about your hometown buddy Deak."

Preston's heart beat fiercely. "Why did I know this was coming?"

"The Ottawa prosecutor is investigating his campaign finances," Jacoby said. "A teller at the bank where he keeps his accounts noticed some strange deposits and started asking questions. It festered for months but when it finally went up the ladder, the law pressed it hard. Deak went in with his attorney last week and admitted to accepting illegal contributions."

"And now that's he's in trouble, he's turning tattletale," Preston said.

"On Mary Lou Harkin's very special friend," Jacoby said. "He claims Breese had sixty thousand dollars delivered to him in April."

"Where?"

"At a Wendy's off I-71, south of Mansfield," Jacoby said. "Deak also taped his phone calls with Breese without telling him. He's got Breese rambling on at length about needing to find something on you. Up in your district and in Columbus."

"Do your sources know who dropped the money for Breese in Mansfield?"

Jacoby hesitated again. "I don't want to upset you, because I think you're acquainted with her."

"Go on."

"Deak's pick-up man described her as short, wiry, in her mid-thirties. With a nice head of dark, thick hair. We can't get a positive ID but we're virtually certain it was Lindy Trego."

"I haven't seen her around since you broke your story on Breese."

"She got a lawyer and went underground. She's working at the Department of Liquor Control in Columbus."

Preston mind was spinning rapidly in several directions. He couldn't keep his thoughts or emotions in check any longer. "I hope you're giving this to me straight," he said. "I'm going to check it out as best I can."

"When have I ever been *anything* but straight with you?"

Preston thought to himself: never. She had kept his name out of every *Citizen* story. She'd never lied, deceived, or played him for anything. Could he say the same about anybody else involved in the situation?

"Good luck in Washington," he said.

"Keep fighting the good fight, Mr. CLEAN. Don't ever, *ever* give up."

*   *   *

The week after the election, Preston went to the Hyatt on Capitol Square to participate in a symposium sponsored by the *Citizen*. Sharing a podium with ten lawmakers, reporters and lobbyists, he overcame an attack of stage fright and offered his guarded perspective on the prospects for tax reform in the lame duck, the looming transfer of power in the House, and life in the era of CLEAN.

True to her word, Jacoby had quit her job and left town. She was not in attendance. Neither were the Speaker, Breese or Zinn. But more than two hundred interested parties were, and it was a heady experience to have a couple of dozen of them make an effort to seek him out, say hello and wish him well.

At the end of the program, a cluster of lobbyists converged on him, eager to continue discussions. When he broke free of them after nearly an hour, he left the Square and drove his Taurus five miles up the river to the Department of Liquor Control, a drab, low stucco building on the edge of a limestone quarry. He went into the reception area, gave his name and title to a man behind a glass shield, and asked to see Lindy Trego.

He wasn't sure what would happen next. As the man made two short phone calls and eyed him nervously, Preston wondered if he'd crossed the line again and put himself in yet another situation where his temper might explode. It was a scene he'd been hoping against hope to avoid. But he couldn't find out where she lived, and she wouldn't return his calls, and he was not going to gain any measure of closure or satisfaction until he met her face-to-face and had it out.

Two large male security guards came down a long hallway toward him. At the last moment, a heavyset man in shirtsleeves popped out of a door and joined them. He greeted Preston with a hearty smile.

"Good afternoon, Representative. Welcome to the department."

"Thank you."

"I'm Bob Dane, chief-of-staff for the director. This is something of an awkward situation, but Ms. Trego doesn't wish to see you."

"I've been trying to reach her for several days," Preston said.

"She just got off the phone with her attorney," Dane said.

"It's urgent that I speak with her."

"She doesn't wish to speak with you."

"I'd like to know why not."

"With all due respect, sir, that isn't really our concern."

"Actually, it's my concern."

"We understand the delicacy of the situation."

"I'm a member of the General Assembly."

"Yes, sir."

"One of the people who approves your budget."

"We're aware of that, sir. But if you don't leave on your own accord we'll have no choice but to detain you here and notify law enforcement."

"Am I trespassing?"

"What I'd suggest is that we not find out if you are or not."

Dane, sweating in the overheated lobby, loosened his shirt collar with a grimy hand. Arms crossed, the guards looked blankly at the floor. The man behind the shield sat at rapt attention, ready to spring into action if needed.

With visions of violence dancing in his head, Preston backed away from the group and left the building. Like a quartet of cows, they gathered at the door and stared at him until he was behind the wheel of his Taurus and on his way out of the parking lot.

29

"You can mope like a cur, girlfriend. Or you can make something happen."

On a rain-soaked Thanksgiving afternoon, Breese dove into a brimful plate of turkey and trimmings and tried, yet again, to lift the Speaker out of her funk hole. A week after the election she'd received him briefly in her office in the Center to take possession of three grams, but since then she had not responded to any of his messages. Through ten days of silence he grew fretful. When he heard from two credible friends that he was under investigation by the Ottawa County prosecutor for his dealings with Deak, he became frantic—and confused. He did not know what, if anything, to tell her.

He'd driven to Tomahawk Trail on impulse and surprised her at high noon. She was in her bathrobe at the breakfast table, playing solitaire and poking at a soggy bowl of granola. He convinced her to clean up and get dressed, and they drove thirty miles to a three o'clock serving at the Inn at Cedar Falls in the Hocking Hills. That is where he was working on her, secluded in an upstairs room, away from the flock of diners on the ground floor.

"Get off the mat," Breese said. "We're not finished."

"The Rs are calling all the shots."

"Not yet they aren't."

"I'm rotten bacon that gets dumped down the disposal."

"You stepped up when Vern died."

"No, I didn't," she said. "I got shoved to the front by a gang of guys who didn't want Lynch."

"Held the caucus together for five years."

"Either you're strong enough to hold the majority or you're not."

"You going to shrivel up and die because you lost?"

"I didn't lose," she said. "I got blown off the face of the Earth."

He wondered if she knew that Deak was blabbing. Maybe she knew as much as he did, or more, and had chosen to withhold that information from him. Perhaps she knew nothing. Just a couple of weeks ago, *he* would have told *her* everything. Now, with the trust between them eroding quickly, he was growing more reluctant by the minute to share anything of what he'd learned.

"66 is going to move," he said. "I'm going to help my clients as best I can."

"Do you have any clients left?"

"I've got several." In fact, he only had one, a brother from Bravo Company who owned a string of Laundromats in Clark County and wanted tax abatements for a couple of parcels he was trying to develop. But she didn't need to know that. "Work with me," he said. "There's money to be made before they kick my butt out the door."

"The thought of trying to do tax reform makes me physically ill."

"You're turning the project over to Kimball?"

"Why not?"

"With Zinn at the end of the rostrum, seething like a baboon?"

"Nobody is going to take marching orders from me."

Breese revved up his rallying cry a few more times. She twirled her butter knife in the air, moved her food around on her plate, and stared at the wall. His chest heaved with frustration. He loved the woman. Despite the pain and humiliation she'd heaped on him, he would love her until the day he died and perhaps beyond. But she was disgusting him. There was no shame in defeat. The forces allied against them had been too powerful. Deep down, she knew that. If she couldn't regain a big chunk of fortitude in very short order, she was headed for a breakdown. And he wouldn't be there to save her. He was going to be too busy saving himself.

They finished their meal in virtual silence and drove back to Tomahawk Trail in a pelting rain. The front seat of the Imperial seemed as suffocating as a crypt. He dropped her at the kitchen door and headed north.

*　*　*

The next afternoon, in the bar at the Sandusky Yacht Club, Breese nursed a gin and tonic and watched Preston come at him down the royal blue carpet from the lobby.

As he got close, Breese could see his face clearly. It bore a look of stony outrage, and he realized immediately that Preston knew. Of course he knew. How could he have been so blissfully stupid to think otherwise? If Breese's friends at the *Blade* and the AG's office knew, then Preston had to know. He emptied his glass and braced for a round of nastiness.

"Welcome back to the North Coast," Preston said.

"Always a pleasure."

"Not this time," Preston said.

"No?"

"You lied to me," Preston said. "Right here on this bar stool in July. I asked you straight up, man-to-man, if you funneled money to Deak and you lied to my face."

"Whoa, partner."

"You sent Lindy Trego to Mansfield to make the drop for you," Preston said.

The mention of her name sent a shooting pain up Breese's gut to his heart. "That's the craziest thing I've ever heard," he said.

"And you hired a private eye in Sandusky to root around in my trash. All on her orders."

Breese's armpits were drenched. He felt drops of sweat trickling down his ribcage. "I know Deak's blabbing," he said.

"Mostly about you."

"There's no reason to believe a word he says because he's a bucket of scum. Forget Deak and work with me."

"No."

"Next week in Ways & Means," Breese said. "Kimball is running an amendment for me that creates two tax abatements over in Springfield."

"Is that all you've got left? What happened to Bank One and the Limited and the race track owners?"

"I humbly request your support."

"Go to hell," Preston said.

"I just might, if you give me some help on this."

"I won't support your amendment."

"Think of it as Kimball's, not mine," Breese said. "You going to break your promise to him?"

"I made no promise to Kimball," Preston said. "I haven't heard a word about this until right now."

"That's not his version."

"Then Kimball can go to hell, too."

Breese let out a sigh of disgust. With Deak spilling his guts, the situation was beyond repair. The fact that he'd been fool enough to drive up here and try to fix it was merely a sign of his desperation. If he gave it five or ten years, and both of them were still around, Preston might be able to forgive him for what he'd done. Until that happened, it was pointless to try to make amends.

He paid his tab and went out into the bracing night air. It took him a moment to realize that Preston had followed him into the parking lot. He stood at the back of the Imperial as Breese fiddled with his keys.

"I should have gone to the law months ago and outed the whole lot of you," Preston said.

"But you didn't," Breese said. "There must have been a reason *why* you didn't. Why don't you focus on that?"

"The most despicable thing is siccing Lindy on me," Preston said.

"What do you mean?"

"You put her up to it, didn't you? Paid her to get me into bed."

"Shut your mouth," Breese said. "You've got no right to judge her. Or me."

"The hell I don't." Preston came up the side of the car and into his face. "You're a piece of garbage."

Breese lashed out with his hand and shoved Preston in the chest, knocking him backward. Preston put his right fist over his face and then his left fist, wrapped in a thick glove, came out of nowhere and smacked Breese square in the nostrils. He screamed, fell back against the car door, and slipped slowly to the ground. A minute later, he saw Preston climb into a Taurus and move out of the lot onto Water Street.

He sat on his ass on the slushy pavement, stemming his bleeding as best he could with a handkerchief. His back was bent out of shape. Something was throbbing above his knee. He thought maybe, just maybe, it was time to get out of the business.

*   *   *

Two days later, in the conference room at the Titan Group mansion, Breese faced down Junig and Corrigan again. They had all four of the other partners with them this time, lined up like a firing squad across the side wall, trying not to stare at Breese's crumpled nose and bloated, purple lip.

"We terminated you this morning," Junig said. "You are no longer a member of this firm."

"Who's for me and who's against me?"

"We didn't take a vote," Junig said. "We reached a consensus that this is the best way to handle the situation."

"I admire you deeply," Corrigan said. "I have the greatest respect in the world for your talents. But you're doing too much damage."

"Can't you wait until the lame duck adjourns?"

"Your aroma is pungent," Junig said. "We need to fumigate now."

"You're screwing me over," Breese said. "I've got business to finish."

The black partner Thompson cleared his throat. "So do we," he said. "We've got reps who won't talk to us because you're still here."

"Who?"

"Torp is our main concern."

"Torp is a paranoid creep and a bully," Breese said. "He's overreacting."

"I happen to agree with you," Thompson said. "Most of us do."

"Why don't you tell him that?"

Thompson shrugged his shoulders. "It's not our job to tell the next Speaker of the House how to *feel*."

"What am I doing that's so horribly wrong?"

Junig's eyes twinkled with delight. "We'll let the prosecutors and the AG tell you that," he said. "Here, up in Ottawa County. Wherever else you've been pulling this shit all these years."

Thompson took a step off the wall and bellowed at Breese. "What makes you think you can ship dirty money to Deak behind *our* backs?"

"Take the weekend and move your belongings out," Junig said.

"If you dragged *our* money into this, you're going to jail," Thompson said.

The partners filed out of the room in silence, all of them averting his eyes. Breese sat at the table, simmering in silent rage. Ten minutes later, he locked his office door, left the mansion and eased his aching body up State Street toward a Greek restaurant where he often ate lunch. As he came to the entrance, a savage pain exploded in his jaw and ripped down his left side all the way to his waist. Sweat cascaded down his temples, and then a load of vomit exploded out of his mouth and onto the sidewalk.

With alarming clarity, he realized what was happening to him. There was not a second to waste. He thanked God or his mother in heaven or whatever force it was that had put him at this exact point, at this exact moment in time.

Breathing slowly and moderately hard, he wobbled across State Street and into the emergency room at Grant Hospital. Inside the door, an attendant hailed him from behind a counter.

"Do you need to be seen?"

"Son, I think I might be about to die."

He crumpled to the floor and blacked out.

                    *   *   *

He awoke in a bed next to a window, five or six stories in the air, looking west toward the Square and the huge construction cranes hovering over the Statehouse. He was covered with swatches of tape and strands of black plastic, and an IV was strapped to his left hand above his knuckles.

A young, red-headed nurse came into the room, smiled, and touched his arm. "Mr. Breese. Good morning."

"What's going on?"

"You had a heart attack," she said. "But we got hold of you quick and it looks like you're going to be OK."

He stared at the IV. "What are you feeding me?"

"Nitroglycerin," she said. "To dilate your blood vessels."

"How long am I going to be here?"

"Probably several days."

"Can you track down my phone?"

"Don't worry, it's safe with me," the nurse said.

"Please, honey. I'm in urgent need of my phone."

"I'm afraid you can't have it just yet," the nurse said. "Rest now, Mr. Breese. Just rest."

30

On the morning of the first day of the lame duck, Zinn got out of bed in his house in Massillon at five o'clock. He showered, shaved, and dressed, kissed his sleeping wife and babies farewell, and drove 120 miles in a pre-dawn drizzle to Columbus. Shortly before eight, he arrived at his office on the twelfth floor of the Center. After leaving a sheaf of documents on his secretary's desk and a voice mail message with his attorney, he took the elevator alone to the thirty-first floor.

When the door opened, he saw that the main dining room at Christopher's was nearly empty, and he was disappointed. He'd been hoping for a larger audience. Under the old order the place would have been packed to the gills. But this was the first session of the CLEAN era. Lobbyists and lawmakers alike were legally required to disclose the cost of *all* meals given and received— regardless of amount. That prospect undoubtedly had scared off a horde of regulars—at least for the time being.

He glanced into the alcove where the Speaker kept a private table. There was a place set, but no one was there. He slipped inside and out of view. Dropping to a knee, he pulled up his pant leg to make sure the photograph of his mother that he'd strapped to his calf with duct tape was secure. Then he said a prayer, crossed himself, and walked to the entrance to the dining room.

A dozen or so people observed him. A few waved hello. The maitre-d' scurried up and asked if he wanted to sit down and have something to eat. He ignored them all and fixed his eyes on the big plate glass window in the far back corner of the room.

He burst into a run, reaching full speed in a few seconds. A waitress screamed. A bulky man stood up, lunged awkwardly into the aisle and tried to tackle him. Zinn shoved a stiff arm into his chest and sent him crashing backward into a table.

As he approached the window he leaned in with his head and shoulders and spread his arms behind him, like a sprinter at the wire. He sprang off the floor, hit the glass full force, and crashed through.

In the skyscrapers encircling the Square, he saw jagged streaks of windows lighted up in the foggy darkness. He saw a fountain of blood gushing out of his neck and mouth and drenching his finest suit. He saw concrete pavement rising up to greet him at a hundred miles per hour and that was the last thing he ever saw.

*   *   *

Five hours after Zinn's body hit the ground on State Street next to the Center, the Speaker canceled all House committee hearings and floor sessions for the remainder of the week. The President of the Senate quickly followed suit.

The Statehouse community had never witnessed a performance suicide by one of its own. The luridness of the event intensified with each new revelation: Zinn's bitter, profane note, which he'd mailed the day before he died to each member of the House and to Jana Jacoby in Washington; a fresh report in the *Citizen* that he was about to be indicted by a federal grand jury in Cleveland for accepting bribes in connection with his tax reform bill; gruesome details about the state of his brutalized corpse, including an unconfirmed report that two hours after the death plunge, a janitor hoisted on a scaffold had scraped an eyeball off a window pane outside the tenth floor.

On Saturday, in the middle of a blinding snow, he was buried next to his mother at a private family ceremony at Quaker Hill Cemetery in Limaville.

When the lame duck reconvened three days later, a noon memorial service was held at Trinity Episcopal Church, across Third Street from the Statehouse. In a pew in the middle of a nave filled beyond capacity, Hyams found scant solace in the homilies of the House chaplain and the smarmy speeches offered up in remembrance of Zinn's troubled soul.

It did not seem odd to her that a man so despised in life could, in death, inspire such an elaborate display of grief. That was the way of the world; it was even more the way of those in public life. Nor was it surprising that beneath the pious façade, an ugly partisan struggle was underway over the question of which party had the right to appoint Zinn's successor, who would serve out the remainder of the lame duck in his place. The language appeared to side with the Rs. But that would have to be verified quickly by lawyers or, God forbid, judges, if the argument dragged on that long.

What *was* remarkable was the spirited resurrection of Zinn's tax reform bill. To remove the sordid link to the deceased, all of the major components of 66 had been neatly transferred under Kimball's guidance into 303, a simple housekeeping item whose original purpose had been to change the filing deadlines for the county lodging tax. Against all odds, the retooled vehicle was picking up support on many fronts, and seemed to have a real chance of winning House and Senate approval in the days remaining before final adjournment.

As she filed down the center aisle at the end of the service, she spotted Preston out ahead of her in the vestibule, pensive as usual, slipping his arms into an expensive-looking black overcoat. Their eyes met, and she moved through the crowd toward him. They left the church together and walked down Broad Street past the bulldozers and cranes on the Statehouse lawn.

"I just wanted to let you know you're wrong," Preston said.

"What do you mean?"

"The Speaker does go after her own," Preston said. "She went after me."

He launched into his tale of betrayal, the same one he'd fixated on in April. But this time there were more details: the amount of money exchanging hands, the time and date of the rendezvous, the tapes Deak had of his phone conversations with Breese.

Preston even knew the names of the prosecutors and investigators working the case.

The story carried such a ring of authenticity that it nearly brought her to tears. From the moment he broached the subject, she was virtually certain that Mary Lou and Evan had done what he accused them of doing. She knew both of them too well to think otherwise. The purpose of concealing her conclusions from Preston had been to steer him away from the vicious cycle of attack of recrimination that was destroying the caucus. But this morning, with a thousand fingers of suspicion pointed at Mary Lou, and Evan apparently on the verge of indictment, she felt foolish—and ashamed of herself—for defending their honor.

"Stop fighting yesterday's battles," Hyams said.

"I haven't won yet."

"The only ones still standing are you and Torp," she said. "Who says you haven't won?"

"I put team first," Preston said. "Laid the negativity aside. And all the while, this woman is playing me like a fiddle."

"Look to the future, Jack." Hyams said. "303 is ready to come out of Ways & Means. Vote for it."

"I will not vote for 303," Preston said. "And I'm not betraying all that is good and right and just in the world if I don't. No matter what she's telling everybody."

"This is not her finest moment," Hyams said. "It's her last gasp of power and she looks pathetic."

"She's trying to turn this vote into a litmus test. It's beyond ridiculous."

"303 *does* help wage earners and small businesses."

"I know it does."

"More than it helps corporations or public utilities or politicians."

"They made out all right, too."

"There you go again," Hyams said. "Off the path into the wilderness, in search of the perfect bill."

"The giveaways to special interests are obscene."

"303 has flaws," Hyams said. "But CLEAN had flaws and you voted for that."

They arrived on the wide sidewalk in front of the Center. Workers bustled in and out of the revolving doors. Before she turned to go inside, she grabbed Preston by the arm and squeezed hard. "Let it go, Jack."

"Why should I let it go?"

"You know this is a good bill," Hyams said. "But you're going to vote no anyway—because you're angry at her?"

"Maybe, maybe not."

"Think it *all* the way through—A to Z."

"I'll do my best to put personal feelings aside," Preston said. Somehow, she didn't think so.

31

Eight days after the memorial service for Zinn, Preston left the Center at four o'clock, walked across the upper level of the underground garage, and flashed his House member ID to a Highway Patrol trooper at the basement entrance to the Statehouse.

The trooper waved him through a sliding glass door. He picked his way across a slippery, makeshift pathway of wooden planks and past yards of exposed brickwork that gave the place the look of a wine cellar in the bowels of a castle. Then he went up a stone stairwell to the main construction zone in and around the rotunda.

There, beneath the giant scaffolds erected for the re-plastering phase of the renovation, Torp was waiting for him, a winter overcoat slung over his arm. He cast a bemused eye on Preston and ambled across a dirty canvas tarp to shake his hand.

"Greetings, Jack. This isn't exactly that cup of coffee I promised you this summer but I guess it's close enough, what do you think?"

"I must say you're taking paranoia to a whole new level."

"You can never be too careful," Torp said. "And there are some guys I prefer to meet face-to-face. Even if we have to hide."

"Congratulations on your triumph," Preston said. "You did good."

"Congratulations to *you*, Jack."

"So good I take it you didn't invite me here to ask me to switch parties."

Torp gazed upward at the workers high on the scaffolds, inside the dome, scratching old plaster off the walls. "That's not in the script anymore," he said. "Not that I personally wouldn't welcome you. But some of my young braves would be upset. Sleeping with the enemy and all that."

"I understand."

He made eye contact with Preston and touched him lightly on the elbow. "I do have an urgent request to make of you, though. Keep voting no on 303. On this monstrosity being concocted by our deranged colleagues."

"I'm undecided on 303."

"We can still kill it."

"I'm not sure I want to kill it."

Torp grimaced. "You voted no in Ways & Means," he said. "And on the floor. If there'd been a couple more profiles in courage on your side, we could have slain this beast right there and been home in time for Christmas. So why are you on the fence now?"

"Pressure from my leadership."

Torp gave him a sniggering look. "These are the same folks who just took you from 54 seats to 39?"

"Except for her, they're all coming back next year," Preston said. "I need them."

"Whatever in the world for? I'll tell you from experience, they can't do much for you."

"I need to read the conference committee report," Preston said "Find out what stayed in the bill and what got yanked out."

"You and I won't really *know*, Jack. Until a month from now, after the lawyers pore over it and figure out what it all means. That's what disgusts me. We've got three senators and three reps locked up in some room right now, filling stockings for every special interest in the state. When they're done, we'll get 300 pages of glop dumped in our laps half an hour before the vote."

"And be expected to make an informed decision," Preston said. "Which we *cannot* do."

There was a cry of warning from the scaffolds, and they dodged a fluffy stream of plaster falling from the dome.

Torp kicked dust off his shoes. "The process is a disgrace," he said. "We pass this load of manure and ship it to the Senate and they look at it for—what? Five minutes?"

"Just long enough to fold in all the agreed-on language."

"I'm out to kill this conference report," Torp said. "Would you like to join me in my effort?"

"I don't know," Preston said. "I'll have to surprise you again."

"It's the perfect symbol of everything I detest about this system," Torp said. "This isn't about politics anymore. Or party."

"It never was."

"It's about forty-six of my guys and as many of yours as I can get giving this town a nice, stiff wake-up call for January."

"No more business as usual," Preston said. "Isn't that the line?"

"Go ahead and smirk," Torp said. "I can't blame you. But this is a defining moment for me. I can *feel* it."

"Don't you have any language in 303?"

"Many of my friends are quite pleased with the bill," Torp said. "But every once and a while you have to step back and see the bigger picture and disappoint your friends."

"I already have."

"Emotions are raw. I understand."

"Extremely."

"An army of you aren't coming back," Torp said. "And Zinn has unhinged people."

"Zinn and the fact that you get to replace him with one of your own."

"We get the seat because our guy beat Zinn in the election last month," Torp said. "I can see why it rankles, but the Constitution is clear as a bell."

Torp put on his overcoat and asked Preston to walk him over to the Third Street entrance. They left the construction zone and passed through the Atrium. When they got close to the door leading into the Senate Building, there was a knot of staffers thirty yards out ahead of them, talking in feverish tones at the top of a stairway. Before they could be spotted, Torp took Preston's arm and pulled him behind a limestone pillar.

"I won't forget a no vote," Torp whispered. "Just to make that perfectly clear."

"What are you saying?"

"I'll be seeking input from select members of the minority," Torp said. "You probably don't believe that, but wait and see. You're already on my short list—and a no vote on this will push you to the top."

"Are you ready to be Speaker?"

"Can I be totally honest with you?"

"Aren't you always?"

"I'm scared."

"Of what?"

"This term limits nonsense," Torp said. "Eight years and out *sounds* good. The problem is, it's not going to *work*. People will get here on Monday and start looking for their next job on Tuesday, before they even figure out where the bathroom is."

"I thought you were a strong supporter of term limits."

Torp smiled. "I put up a good front to keep the loonies and lunatics happy," he said. "But as far as I'm concerned, we've *always* had term limits. They're called elections."

"You term-limited a lot of guys last month."

"Maybe I did them a favor," Torp said. "Because this place is going to be different. *Everybody* is a general now, CEO of Me First, Incorporated. You can't run a House that way."

Torp peeked around the pillar. The group at the top of the stairs had dispersed. He and Preston walked again, and when they reached the east side of the Senate Building, he stopped and put on earmuffs and a pair of gloves. "There you have it," he said. "My shocking confession of the day. I'm going to swear you to secrecy and be off to church."

"Are you praying for the death of 303?"

Torp fiddled with his ear muffs to get them on tight. "I'm not sure the Lord cares if 303 lives or dies," he said. "All I'm asking Him for tonight is extra strength."

He went out the door to Third Street. Preston went back to the garage, got into his Taurus and drove to the Holiday Inn. On his voice mail, there was a message from the Speaker's office.

She wanted to see him. That was a welcome development, because he wanted to see her, too. He called back and made an appointment.

32

The next morning, Preston entered the Union Plaza via a little-used door on Gay Street and took the elevator to the eleventh floor. He walked through the stillness of the hallway to the Speaker's suite and gently knocked three times.

There was no response.

He knocked harder, and again no one answered. He turned back toward the elevator, and as he did the door lurched open.

"Jack—good morning."

The Speaker stood in the hallway, wearing some kind of kimono or night robe, a piece of sheer blue fabric that hung on her gaunt body like a potato sack. She was barefoot. Her eyes were bloodshot, her hair a gnarled mess, her face covered with globs of moisturizing cream.

"Excuse me," Preston said. "I can come back later."

"No, come in. Let's get this over with."

Hugely ill at ease, but determined to see his mission through, he followed her into the suite. In the outer room, three plastic cartons full of household and kitchen items were piled by the door, and a couple of half-packed suitcases lay open on the couch. Several paintings had been taken off the walls and stacked in a corner.

"I'm afraid I overslept," she said. "Grab a cup of coffee if you want."

He did. She went into the bedroom and shut the door. A minute later, he heard what sounded like the contents of a medicine cabinet crashing onto a tile floor. He moved to the bedroom door, intending to knock and ask if she was all right, then changed his mind. In a hardback chair at the coffee table, he perused a scrapbook of clips and mementoes tracing the accomplished career of Mary Lou Harkins: foot soldier in the War on Poverty, field director for RFK's presidential campaign, first woman president of Chillicothe City Council, chair of the House Aging & Housing Committee, Majority Whip, Speaker of the House.

At the back of the scrapbook, tucked into a plastic sleeve, was a black-and-white headshot of a quite young Zinn, looking straight at the camera's eye. He looked twenty or so, with a wild head of curly black hair and some kind of chain medallion around his neck. In place of his trademark smirk was what appeared to be a genuine smile. It seemed to stand for the proposition that Zinn, for at least a single moment in his life, might have been happy.

She emerged from the bedroom, haphazardly dressed and coiffed. A couple of strands of blue yarn or string were stuck in her hair. One of the buttons on her blouse was open, exposing a swatch of flesh. She gave Preston the once over and tossed a nod of approval at his yellow tie and freshly-shined wingtips. Then she went to the picture window and stood in the light of first dawn, staring down at the Statehouse.

"The Senate is going to approve the conference committee report on 303 this morning," she said.

"Is that definite?"

She nodded. "They'll send it to us and go home. We're going to the floor for a straight up or down vote."

"When?"

"As soon as possible," she said. "I want to go home, too."

"Your defeat must have been crushing," Preston said. "You have my deepest condolences."

She shot a bitter smile at him. "The point of politics is to survive," she said. "I didn't."

"I'm sorry it's ending like this for you," he said. "All the backstabbing and fingerpointing. And Zinn."

"He was troubled from the day he was conceived," she said. "Most of it was in his genes. But if his father hadn't walked out on the family when he was a month old, I think he would have been all right."

"You've known him that long?"

"I changed his diapers, taught him how to read, found him a home after his mother died."

"I knew you were close," Preston said. "I had no idea you were that close."

"He's ripped a giant hole in my heart and I'm never going to get over it," she said. "The only goal I've got now is to leave office on as high a note as I can."

"To do right by him?"

"No, Jack. I'm furious at him for what he did."

"Excuse me."

"I will never forgive him as long as I live," she said. "All I want to do is pass this bill. Because when all the grief and anger and disgust burns away, that's what we're going to be left with."

"Why is 303 moving?"

"Because enough people—*barely* enough—have more reasons to vote for it than against it."

"Would this be happening if Zinn were alive?"

"Why are you speculating?" she said. "The bill is in front of us now. That's all that matters."

"303 is the end game, then."

"Yes, it is," she said. "And I very much need your vote."

"I'd like to give it to you."

The Speaker came away from the window. She pulled a big painting of a zebra off the wall and laid it in the corner with the others. "Haven't you made your point by voting no twice?" she said. "Shaken your fist at all the people you need to shake your fist at?"

"I don't know."

"We've offered you whatever you want and you keep turning us down."

"My vote is not for sale—or rent," Preston said. "I've been voting no because I have serious concerns about the bill."

"What are they?"

"A billion dollars of corporate welfare," Preston said.

"I hate that more than you do," she said. "But we need every dime of it to hold the support of the Senate."

"Everything important happens in the dark," he said. "The rank-and-file have no input."

"If you don't matter, why am I standing here begging for your vote?"

She yanked a painting of a Ferris wheel off the wall. "I thought you cared about the middle class and small businesses."

"I do."

"We're cutting property taxes for seniors," she said. "Ending the income tax completely for almost a million low income wage earners."

"Yes, we are."

"The S corporation loopholes are being slashed," she said. "Phone companies are going to fund 9-1-1. Schools will be made whole for the revenue they lose from tax abatements. Do you think there's a snowball's chance in hell of *any* of that happening next year?"

"I don't suppose there is, no."

She put the Ferris wheel painting in the corner and sat down across from him on the couch. "So what is your hang up?" she said.

"My hang-up is you," he said.

She jerked upright and fixed her eyes on him. He glanced at her hands and was shocked to see the tips of all her fingers chewed to the quick, the skin around the nails as pink as raw hamburger.

"How can I get you over your hang-up?" she said.

"I'd like to ask you some questions," Preston said. "To clear the air."

"Ask me anything you want."

"If you tell me the truth, I'll vote for 303."

"Fair enough."

"Did you collect honorariums at breakfasts with Breese's clients when he was working as a solo lobbyist?"

"A dozen times or more," she said. "We did exactly the same thing Robby got nailed to the cross for. We were just more polite about it."

"Why did you and leadership stop?"

"It got to the point where we didn't need honorariums anymore," she said. "We passed the opportunities off to the chairmen and the rest of you."

"Did Breese hire a private eye up in my district to dig up dirt on me? And pay Lindy Trego to do the same thing in Columbus?"

"I presume he paid her, yes."

"Did he send her to Mansfield to pass sixty thousand dollars to Deak in April?"

"That, too."

"All at your direction?"

She nodded at him. "I was mad at you," she said. "I didn't like the things you said about me."

The swiftness and clarity of her confession stunned him. He had come to the suite to find out everything she had just told him. But he'd expected her to evade, shade, equivocate—or deny everything altogether. He squirmed in his chair in baffled silence, then went to the kitchenette and poured another cup of coffee.

"Why did you tell me all that?" Preston said.

She shrugged her shoulders. "A deal is a deal," she said. "And I know my secrets are safe with you. As much as you despise me, as much contempt as you have for the way I've behaved, you're too deep into this business to go out and blab now."

"Deak taped his conversations with Breese," Preston said. "He's given them to the Ottawa prosecutor. Do you know that?"

"Yes, I do."

"They're working with the AG's office. And Richland County has gotten involved because that's where the money changed hands."

"Evan is easy pickings these days," she said.

"He could be indicted by the end of the year," Preston said. "Then the trail leads to you."

"The trail may lead to me, but nobody is going to walk down it,"she said. "Because I'm finished. I'm no threat to anybody anymore. All this noise about all the horrible things I've done is going to die down very quickly."

"Why did you go after me with such a vengeance?"

"You opened a can of worms that didn't need to be opened."

"Is the House better off with CLEAN or without it?"

"You'll be here to find out," she said. "I think you'll discover the old way wasn't so bad."

"After all you did to hurt me, you had the audacity to turn around and ask me to raise money for you."

"Did I manipulate you, Jack? Mess with your head and make you feel guilty and lure you in?"

"Big time."

"Why didn't you just tell me to go to hell?"

"I don't know why."

"I'll tell you why—because you *wanted* to be lured in. You arrived two years ago condescending as hell. Government is a joke, run by fools and crooks. But now that you're *here,* you realize the setup isn't nearly as awful as you thought it was. And you want to stick around for a while. Am I right?"

She fidgeted with her hair and jewelry, then went into the bedroom. He could see that she'd been sapped by her confessions, and by the talk of defeat and death. She was finished with him. He stood up and moved toward the door.

She shouted at him from the bathroom. "Have I answered all your questions?"

"Yes, you have."

"Can I count on your vote then?"

"Yes, you can."

"I don't think I'll be seeing you again," she said.

"And yes, Madame Speaker, you're right about me," Preston said. "I do want to stick around for a while."

He waited a moment to see if she might respond. All he heard was the sudden rush of water, running full force into the bathtub. He closed the door softly as he left.

33

At three o'clock on Christmas Eve afternoon, Breese eased his body gingerly up the stairs from the underground parking garage and headed across High Street toward the Departments Building. Frail after twenty days on his back, and twenty-five pounds lighter from a fruit and vegetable diet, he felt a surge of dizziness and stopped to steady himself against a parking meter.

The doctors had released him from the hospital after four nights and told him to go home and stay there. He'd followed their orders until today. That was easy enough to do because home was a heck of a good place to be—away from prosecutors, media, creditors, ex-clients, ex-wives and the rest of the mob that wanted a piece of his hide.

But with the final floor session of the 120th General Assembly underway—and word coming from the half dozen people still talking to him that the vote on 303 would be tight as a drum—he'd piled into his Imperial and driven downtown. Through with his efforts to win approval for the conference report, he simply wanted to be present in the House chamber one last time.

On the corner of State and High outside the Center, a legless man in a wheelchair hawked ornaments and candy canes out of a cardboard box. Further down the hill, a section of State near the curb was covered with a bushy holiday wreath, complete with red bows and ribbons. Underneath the wreath was a tattered bouquet of roses. He suddenly realized that this was the spot where Zinn's body had landed.

He looked up. It was a straight, sheer drop to the ground from the thirty-first floor. There were no ledges or protrusions on the building. Zinn must have picked this path to make certain his descent was full and complete.

The gruesomeness of the image made him blanch. It was a sickening shame about the wife and children he'd left behind, and the havoc he'd wreaked on Mary Lou and the caucus. The only good thing about Zinn hurling himself out of Christopher's was that it had revived a better than decent bill that had been nearly suffocated by scandal. In death, he was giving the Ds a parting shot at something resembling redemption before they descended into the minority.

Inside the chamber, the visitors and press gallery was packed. Breese's pale skin and withered frame drew stares as he edged into a line of lobbyists standing along the back wall. Several minor bills had been processed, floor debate on 303 was underway, and Torp was at his microphone, condemning it as a mix of arrogance, greed and disrespect for the proud people of the state. In their rows, the members shifted like sullen cattle. On the dais, the Speaker stared impassively out at the group, her croquet mallet of a gavel in hand.

She wasn't communicating with him anymore, undoubtedly on the advice of her lawyers. There had been several calls the first week after he'd gotten home from the hospital, then nothing. Their estrangement was total, their separation complete. And if she was aware of his presence in the chamber now, she wasn't letting on.

She must have found someone else to secure her treats. Or perhaps she was substituting with alcohol or Valium, or even going cold turkey. It distressed him that things had gotten so out of hand on that front. She'd never had a problem with the stuff until the last year or so, then all of sudden she couldn't stop. He feared for her condition. But it was no longer his place to intervene.

Torp finished his diatribe. Lynch rebutted on behalf of the Ds, and as the vote approached Breese felt confident of victory. His brother from Bravo Company had promised him a bonus of ten large if the conference report passed with his tax abatements intact. With medical and legal bills mounting and his income stream virtually gone, it was money he desperately needed merely to keep his head above water. And it looked as though he was going to get it. According to the most accurate count he could muster, Torp had 42 votes from his own caucus and four or five or six discontented Ds, and that was all. His effort to derail the thing was going to come up short.

Apparently the clincher was Preston. The skinny on Mr. CLEAN was that he was now a yes, a *definite* yes. Not that he would know first hand, because after their dust-up in Sandusky, Jack had cut him off cold. But in the last two days someone in leadership must have gotten to him, talked some sense into his head, and flipped him around with—what?

Breese had no idea. He doubted if anyone else did, either.

The Speaker called for the House to proceed to vote, and on the first light-up, he scanned the big electronic board for the key players. His knees went weak when he saw red next to Preston's name. A couple of young guys along the wall gasped, and one of them cried out "green, Jack, go green!" But when the final light-up locked in ten seconds later, Preston's red remained.

The motion to approve the conference committee report had failed—49 yes, 50 no.

There was silence, then a rumble of anger and confusion. A member up front Breese couldn't recognize screamed for a motion to reconsider. A group in the back screamed no. The leadership team assembled briefly at the dais, then the Speaker slammed her gavel down for the last time and pronounced the House adjourned.

Breese left the Departments Building as quickly he could, moving through the crowded concourse without speaking to anyone. He was through with the place, his spectacular run ending in a sad and ugly way. But he was astonished how at little remorse he felt. That, he knew, would come later. His priority now was to get healthy and prepare himself to fend off whatever the world was going throw at him.

Up on High Street, the legless man waved a bunch of candy canes in the air. Breese handed him a ten and bought two—one for Mary Lou, one for Lindy. Not that he'd be seeing either of them again, except perhaps in a courtroom somewhere. They were three losers in limbo, clinging to their lawyers, waiting for the next piece of sky to fall on their heads.

The legless man lit a cigarette and puffed hard to keep the ember going in the wind. "Are you finished with the people's business?" he said.

"We are finished and gone to heaven," Breese said.

That got the man giggling. "I'll tell you something," he said. "Politics don't have much to do with heaven. Politics is bunk."

"It is."

"Politicians are nothing but a pack of thieves."

"They are."

"I've been on this corner twenty years," the man said. "Faces come, faces go. They all look pretty much the same to me. No matter who's in and who's out, the little people get screwed."

Breese gave the man another ten and bought two more candy canes, one for each of his daughters. "I think you're onto something," he said.

The man reached inside his coat and stuffed the bill into his shirt pocket. "If voting could really *change* anything, it would be illegal," he said. "There'd be a man outside the booth pointing a rifle at you, telling you to move on."

"You're right about that," Breese said.

"Aren't I now?"

"Yes you are," Breese said. "You're absolutely right."

the end